"Scared Hitless"

"A Lemon Drop Martini Club Novel"

By Carolyn Anderson Jones

*This book is dedicated to
Cindy, Kathryn, and Darcie*

"Here's to your liver, lover!"

Prologue

When I was seven, I watched my best friend, Catherine, fall off a swing on our school playground and do a face plant in the hard gravel. It was the 1950s, and we didn't have soft green grass around our two-story, white clapboard schoolhouse. Dirt, gravel, a few weeds, and a cracked sidewalk leading up to the front door of the Louisville Elementary School was the "Martha Stewart" landscaping we all grew up with and loved.

I panicked when I saw Catherine fall, but seeing her accident wasn't the only cause for my upset. Another cause was the premonition I had of the accident moments before it happened, and then watching it come true. But my *biggest* panic was I didn't want any of the boys to see Catherine's panties.

It was hard being a girl in the 1950s. We had to wear dresses to school everyday. No shorts, leggings, or jeans for females back then. Even in the harsh Colorado winters, we had to wear dresses. And it was tough trying to have fun on our old playground equipment—the swings, slides, merry-go-rounds, monkey bars, and seesaws—while holding your dress down.

I knew Catherine could handle a bloody nose, loose tooth, or scraped knee, but the constant teasing if the boys saw her polka-dotted panties would be pure hell. All we'd hear the rest of the day would be, "I saw London, I saw

France, I saw Catherine's underpants!" So I pushed my panic aside, knocked a few guys to the ground, and rushed to help her up before they could see what happened.

As it turned out, Catherine managed to fall flat on her stomach and only knocked the wind out of her lungs and skinned her face up a little. Somehow, while careening through the air, she was able to grab her dress and cover her ass before she hit the ground. Now that's what I call multitasking 1950s style. We didn't have a nurse in our small-town school, so Catherine was sent to be checked out by our second-grade teacher.

Me? I, Constance Canary Woods, got sent to the principal's office for knocking the guys on their butts, the big whiny babies.

But all in all, I didn't think it was such a bad deal, because that day I learned I had a special gift—premonitions. I have no control over my gift. Just like I have no control over my middle name. My mother was really into birds, so my two sisters and I are blessed with bird middle names. Rachel Robin is the oldest, I'm stuck in the middle, and Whitney Wren is the baby. I always felt I got the raw end of the deal because Robin and Wren are almost normal names. But Canary?

Oh well, back to my premonitions. Over the years I learned I can never tell when one is going to happen, or who or what it's going to be about. They suddenly hit me out of the clear blue, and sometimes I have time to warn people, and sometimes I don't. Fortunately, they're never about catastrophic or historic events, like earthquakes, hurricanes, or the death of a famous person, like Elvis. They're simply premonitions about people, places, and things close to me in my own little world.

I also learned early on that talking about my premonitions creeps people out, so basically I keep that secret pretty much to myself and a few close friends, like Catherine.

That was over fifty years ago, and if nothing else, having the middle name of Canary helped me develop a tough skin, a good sense of humor, and a great right hook. Maybe I didn't get such a raw deal after all.

ONE

Deep in the shadows of a deserted, dark alley, across the street from a rundown topless club, two men stood side by side watching the door as patrons staggered out into the warm Denver night.

Paper rustled as the larger of the two reached in his shirt pocket and pulled out a picture. He turned on a small penlight and studied the picture for a few seconds before returning it to his pocket. As he switched off the light, darkness once again permeated the alley.

Tomas Rodriguez, the big man with the picture, was getting antsy. This job was supposed to be an easy-in, easy-out hit, but it was turning into one big cluster fuck. He should be in the private jet heading back to Columbia and his beautiful Elena by now.

"Why do ya keep looking at that picture?" the smaller man next to him whispered. "I know who we're supposed to whack."

Tomas turned his head, and his dark, steely eyes glinted from the glow of the dim streetlights as he looked at the dead body that lay in the alley behind them.

"Yeah, well then why did I waste a bullet on the wrong guy, you stupid shit *gringo*."

The malice in Tomas's voice was as strong as his Spanish accent, and his sarcasm was not wasted on the smaller guy standing next to him.

The small man, half the size of Tomas, squirmed. It was obvious Tomas made the man nervous with his harsh voice and thick Spanish accent. He ran his slender fingers through his thinning, black hair before answering.

"I already told ya once, it was an honest mistake. That guy looked a lot like our mark, and it was too dark for me to see his face from this angle."

Tomas grunted. This job would've been a lot easier if he could've done it by himself. But his boss, Raul Santiago, the head of the biggest drug cartel in Colombia, told him he had to take the nephew of his friend with him when he made the hit. For what reason, he didn't know, but he learned long ago never to question Raul.

The small man giggled nervously as he pulled a Marlboro out of his pocket and clicked his Bic. "We'll get the SOB the minute he sticks his sneaky head outta the door."

Tomas grabbed the cigarette and lighter, threw them to the ground, and crushed them under his foot.

"No lights. No smoking," he grumbled under his breath.

The small man, Donatello "Dusty" Galucci, shrank back against the wall.

Dusty was the nephew of Rocky Galucci, one of the biggest Mafia crime bosses in the western US. Rocky Galucci and Raul Santiago were secret business partners. Raul supplied drugs to Rocky, and Rocky paid Raul whatever he wanted. It was a great arrangement. No one in the Mafia family knew about it and

Rocky wanted to keep it that way. But a syndicated columnist for the biggest newspaper in the West, the *Denver Advocate*, blew it all sky high, or mile high as the case may be, when she wrote an expose on their connection, and that story hit the streets the day before.

Rocky was not a happy man.

Raul was not a happy man.

Obviously Rocky had a mole in his organization, and it took him all of thirty minutes to find out who it was. Raul insisted he send his top man to take care of the informant, not trusting anyone else to do it. Sensing their relationship was on fragile ground, and not wanting to lose his Colombian connection, Rocky agreed. Within an hour Tomas was on a private jet headed toward Denver.

The only hitch in the whole deal was Dusty. Rocky wanted his nephew to contribute to his organization and learn how to take out a few problems from time to time. Rocky figured he could get the training he needed by assisting Tomas, and talked Raul into letting him tag along.

It would've been a good idea except Rocky didn't realize Dusty was the ten-watt bulb in a five-hundred-watt world. His nephew was not only slow, but also dimwitted and stupid. A fact Tomas picked up on real quick when Dusty fingered the wrong man.

"There he is!" Dusty shook a tobacco-stained finger at a frail figure staggering out of the club.

"You better be right this time, *gringo*, or the next bullet will be for you."

Tomas squinted at the drunk stumbling across the deserted street directly toward them. He nodded in silent agreement as a streetlight flickered across the man's face long enough for him to see it was their mark.

Tomas lifted his gun with the silencer, and when the object of Rocky and Raul's ire was within a few feet of the alley, Tomas called softly to him.

"Hey, *amigo*. Got a present for you."

The man turned, and before the shock of what was about to happen could register in his drunken brain, Tomas pulled the trigger.

"Help me get him into the alley," Tomas demanded, when the man fell to the ground. Dusty grabbed a leg and they pulled him up next to their unfortunate mistake.

"Good job," Dusty exclaimed in an excited whisper. "You got him right between the eyes."

Tomas was hauling ass out of the alley when he noticed his protégé wasn't behind him. He looked back and saw Dusty leaning over the dead informant.

"What the fuck are you doing?" His voice rose in irritation. "We gotta get out of here and fast. *Vamanos*!"

"Just hadda leave a warning note for that Catherine James broad, the one who wrote the story that upset my uncle," Dusty explained with a crooked smile.

9

"*Muerda!*" Tomas hit his forehead with his hand. "I'm outta here, with or without you."

He took off for the car parked around the corner. Dusty hurried after him with a big grin on his face. Next time would be his turn. Whacking people was the easiest job in the world!

TWO

Reaching the age of sixty can be mind-boggling. It was for me. The night of my sixtieth birthday, I dreamed I was Maxine, the cartoon maven who delights everyone with her sarcastic wit on all sorts of Hallmark cards.

There I was, just like the birthday card I received that day, running around imparting my profound wisdom to the entire world with all the blue-haired, polyestered glory I could muster up.

In tan crop pants and white nylon knee-highs, I was chasing some *really* good-looking Chippendale studs around yelling, "Any woman can have the body of a twenty-one-year-old—if she buys him a few drinks first."

I woke up and quickly looked under the covers to make sure I didn't have on white knee-highs. Then I jumped up and checked the mirror to make sure my hair wasn't blue. Thank God, I still had my blonde highlights.

Hey, I'm not a floozy, but I'm not my mother's grandma either. And I don't even come *close* to resembling Maxine. At least not yet.

I believe the latest romance novel I was reading caused my midnight paranoia. That, and the half bottle of red wine I drank while reading it.

In the book, the heroine's mother was portrayed as an interfering sixty-something that lived vicariously through her sexy, thirty-year-old daughter. And she had a mole with a big hair sticking out of it on her upper lip.

All I can say is—bull hockey to all this stereotyping. If I want to live vicariously, I do it through my friend, Catherine. We're both divorced and living *la vida loca*. She's more outgoing than I am, so she signs up with Internet dating services. I don't. I'm afraid I would hook up with a serial killer or rapist, so I only use the Internet for the dot-coms that God intended, like Facebook, Twitter, and Amazon. Okay, and maybe Pinterest.

I have two children and three grandchildren, and I live in my hometown of Louisville, Colorado, on the Front Range between Denver and Boulder. I retired from the world of high finance two years ago and decided I wanted to do something fun. So, I got a part-time job at my favorite women's clothing boutique, Amigas, and I've been working there ever since.

I'm also active. And I don't mean sexually. Necessarily. I mean I work out regularly. I go to yoga classes every Sunday, aerobics at least three times a week, jog on occasion, and ride my horse, Willie, all over the great Rocky Mountains. I could be sexually active. After all, I'm sixty, not dead. But I don't have a lot of time for men in my life right now. Maybe I will when I'm older. Like sixty-one.

A week ago I got a tattoo on my right shoulder. It's three hearts, one for each of my grandchildren, and they think I'm pretty cool. That's me, the cool, tattooed grammy.

I have a bucket list and the number one item will never get crossed off—eat more Ben &

Jerry's Cherry Garcia Ice Cream. I don't want to be on my deathbed and have any regrets—not this girl. Number two on the list is to be part of a flash mob with Catherine. But it has to be a really fun one, like a dance at a major airport, big mall, or maybe even a Hollywood studio, like *The Ellen Degeneres Show*.

Catherine thinks I'm setting my goals a little high here, but she'd go to California with me for that. And someone better come up with one soon, because I don't want to be doing a flash mob to *Dancing With The Oldies* with a group of knobby-kneed geriatrics, even if two of those knees are mine.

Several things on my list are more fantasies than realistic goals, but heck, a girl can dream, can't she? Who wouldn't want to video Mike Rowe while he's filming *Dirty Jobs*? Watching a good-looking, hunk of a man like Mike sweat should be on every woman's list, regardless of how old she is.

I thought about being a cougar, but decided against it. Young eye candy is way too much work. Although I can understand why some women go after the younger guys. Most of the men my age don't look all that healthy. I had a blind date once with a guy who was only a year older than me, but he had a bad back and a big belly, and I think he was on oxygen, because he had those little lines on his face an oxygen mask makes. I think he took it off to go on our date, and I worried all night that he would pass out and I might have to give him CPR. I knew that would never work out. You can't carry an oxygen tank when you're riding a horse or on a mountain bike. That ended my dating experience.

I think of myself as normal, but maybe I use the term "normal" loosely, because I still have those premonitions that started when I was in second grade

My premonitions, so far, haven't been of anyone dying. Mostly they're of people about to have something good, bad, or interesting happen to them. And I never have premonitions about myself. I wish I did because maybe I would've had a premonition about my ex-husband before I married him and found out he was a jerk and was going to leave me for a twenty-five-year-old bimbo on my fiftieth birthday.

My premonitions are strange little things. They're like having a nervous tic or unexpected flatulence. You can't predict or control them. They just happen.

I have several best friends in my life besides Catherine. One is Cynthia, who married one of our classmates and is ten years younger than we are, and another is my neighbor, Marcie. And Marcie's the one I was with when my latest premonition hit.

THREE

Marcie is a part-time school nurse and part-time romance writer. She's forty-seven, has a great sense of humor, and you can discuss anything in the world with her. She's one of those people that when you look in her big brown eyes, you can't help yourself. You blurt out all your deepest secrets, and you know she'll never tell. Or put them in one of her books without your permission.

Besides that, her last name is Wine. How can you not love a neighbor with a last name like that?

Marcie and I are in her backyard, floating around on inflatable lounge chairs in her swimming pool on a gorgeous June afternoon discussing which Hollywood hunks we would like to "do." I don't need to explain that, do I?

"Hugh Grant," Marcie says. "I'd do him in a New York minute."

"Richard Gere," I tell her, taking a sip of my bottled water. "I loved him in that movie with Jennifer Lopez."

"Matthew McConaughey," Marcie sighs. "I'd do him twice."

"Marcie, I'm right here and can hear every word you say."

That's Gavin, Marcie's husband, who floats by on his back.

Gavin is the yin to Marcie's yang, and is the best detective in the Broomfield Police

Department. He works out all the time, so he has well-defined pecs, and thick, wavy blond hair.

"Now, Gav, you know you're irreplaceable. I'm just talking about guys I'd do if something happened to you, God forbid."

If ever there were a perfect couple on this earth, I'd say it's Marcie and Gavin. He's quiet, friendly, with a dry sense of humor and totally the opposite of Marcie.

Marcie is a double chocolate chip frappuccino with extra whipped cream and a double shot of caffeine. Gavin is a bold pick of the day—decaf. I don't think they ever argue—they discuss. And they're totally bonkers about each other even after twenty-five years of marriage. I know this for a fact because I've lived next to them for over twelve years.

Floating in the pool in my coral tankini, with my toenails lacquered to match, I suddenly have a premonition.

I can see Catherine, who's a syndicated columnist for the *Denver Advocate*, going into her editor's office, and he's not happy.

In the haze of my vision, I can see another man looming nearby. He's studying a picture of Catherine, and then he smiles. Real big and real menacing.

"Catherine's in danger!" I gasp as I lurch into the pool and swim for the steps.

"What's going on?" Marcie yells, quickly coming out of the pool behind me. "Did you have one of your premonitions?"

16

"Yes, and it was about Catherine. Something's up and I've got to warn her. I'll call ya later, Marcie."

I grab my suit cover and towel, slip into my sandals, snatch my cell and head for home, punching Catherine's number in while I run.

Catherine's cell goes to voice mail, so I leave her a quick message.

"Call me when you get through with the meeting with your boss," I tell her.

I know that will get her attention because she'll wonder how the heck I know she's having a meeting with her boss. All I can do now is wait for her to call me back, and hope she does before anything bad happens.

When I get home, I run up to my second-floor bedroom and hit the shower. Ten minutes later I'm putting on a pair of white capri pants with a light-blue shirt, and blowing out my curly, shoulder-length hair.

I'm slipping my coral-colored toes into a pair of white sandals when my cell phone rings with the familiar Steppenwolf lyrics, "Get your motor runnin', head out to the highway! Lookin' for adventure, and whatever comes our way!"

It's Catherine.

"Hey, what's up girlfriend?" she asks me. "I got your message. How did you know I was in a meeting with my editor?"

That Catherine, she doesn't miss a thing.

"I had a premonition about you about an hour ago," I tell her. "I saw you go into your boss's office and I sensed you were in danger.

17

We need to get together and talk about this. I don't want to do it over the phone."

"Can you meet me for dinner this evening at Gordon Biersch?" she asks.

"Sure. How about five o'clock? If we get there early, we'll be able to grab a table on the patio. I'll give Cynthia a call and see if she can join us."

"Was it a bad premonition?"

"No, but I definitely sensed you were in danger."

"Ah, man. You're good. There are several things I need to talk to you guys about and get your advice. I hope I'm not in any serious danger, but I would like your opinion on how I should handle some things. I gotta go. I'm late for my next appointment, but we'll talk this evening."

The phone clicks as Catherine hangs up.

FOUR

Catherine and Cynthia beat me to Gordon Biersch at the Flatirons Village in Broomfield.

Catherine waves to me from a patio table when I come down the walk into the restaurant. After we have our group hug, I collapse in a chair across from my two BFFs.

There's a Lemon Drop Martini sitting in front of each of us.

The first thing we do is our usual BFF ritual. We toast each other and sip our martinis. We have our priorities straight.

So here we are. Catherine, who's five foot ten and leggy, with layered brown hair that has highlights and lowlights, and big brown eyes; Cynthia, five foot nine with thick honey-blonde hair, blue-green eyes, and cute freckles dancing across her nose; and me. I can barely reach five foot four, and that's only if I stretch my neck way up.

We all have French manicures courtesy of Cynthia—the best hairdresser and nail tech in the West. Did I mention she does our hair too? No wonder we look like we're sixty going on forty—or at least she makes us feel that way.

Cynthia came into our lives when she married one of our classmates and good friend, Dave. Dave and Cynthia never had any kids, and Dave travels a lot, so that leaves Cynthia with gobs of time to spend with us.

Cynthia looks at me with curiosity. "Catherine tells me you had a premonition about her this afternoon."

"I did, and I know you're in danger, Catherine. I saw you going into your meeting, and I also saw an evil, wicked-looking, menacing man staring at a picture of you. I couldn't tell how close he was to you. He could've been in the same room, across the street, or across town. You know how my premonitions blur together. But I distinctly saw you both, and I *definitely* felt strong danger."

"Oh wow," Cynthia murmurs as she sips her martini. "That is so scary."

Catherine leans toward us and lowers her voice.

"This may have something to do with it. You wouldn't believe what I've been going through the past two days. You know those stories I've been working on about the Galucci family? The first one came out in the paper on Sunday, and yesterday they found my informant shot through the head."

"Omigod," I exclaim. "That's awful."

"Yeah, my informant had a bullet in his head and a note pinned to his shirt. Here's a copy of it."

Catherine hands a piece of paper across the table, and Cynthia and I lean in to read it.

"Tell the James woman to bake off or she's next," I read out loud.

I look at Catherine. "Bake off?"

I can't help it, but visions of Catherine in a tall white chef's hat at a Pillsbury Bake-Off fill my head.

Catherine waves her martini around. "Yeah, the guy can't spell. It's awful. This morning I found this note stuffed in my mailbox." She hands over another piece of paper.

"I'm coming after you so wash your stepsister," I read slowly.

A little giggle escapes my lips. "Sorry, Catherine. I know this is serious, but these notes are hilarious."

"I know. I have a hard time taking them seriously too, even though Jack, my editor, isn't laughing. He found out through his connections that the Galuccis put a contract out on me."

Cynthia and I both gasp.

"Oh, shit! That has to be what my premonition is about. I bet the man I saw is the hit man." My voice is bordering on hysterical.

"What are you going to do?" Cynthia asks.

Then it hits me.

I grab Catherine's hand. "What you're going to do is get out of here," I hiss at her. "You can't be out in the open like this. You could get shot at any time. We've got to leave."

I stand up and reach for my purse.

Catherine pulls me back down in my chair.

"Relax, Constance. It's okay. The hit man is a real loser. He's a stupid airhead they call Dusty. Jack told me he's the nephew of

Rocky Galucci, the big crime boss, and he got his name because all he does is hang around and gather dust. He's a real wimp. The police don't think he's a real threat to me because he has the IQ of an ant. We think he's the one who wrote these notes."

Catherine raises her eyebrows with a thoughtful look.

"But Jack did think it'd be a good idea if I left town for a few days. My second and last article about the Galuccis will be in this Sunday's paper."

I'm stunned.

"Catherine, this is serious! And this Dusty freak knows where you live! I don't care what anyone else thinks—I know you're in danger. What are you going to do?"

"I don't know. The police think all this will blow over in a few weeks and Dusty will lose interest. Maybe my boss is right and I should lie low for awhile—but where would I go?"

We're quiet for a few minutes while we think.

The waiter comes up and we all three jump.

"Whoa! Sorry, ladies. You sure are jumpy, but do you want to order now?"

That's a no-brainer, and we all order house salads and a second Lemon Drop Martini.

Then we sip, and think, and look at one another.

FIVE

Our salads come and we're still sipping and looking at one another.

"Okay, I've got it," I tell my two BFFs. "Catherine, you've got to get out of town and we'll go with you. I'll call Rachel. I don't think anyone is using her house in Grand Lake Village, and we'll go there. It's on the secluded southern shore of the lake, with a big ol' alarm system. Not only that, you can only reach it by boat in the summer, or snowmobile in winter. You should be safe there. Plus, it'll be fun. We can have a mini-vacation."

I stop myself. Where's my brain? A mini-vacation? Catherine is getting death threats, and here I'm thinking about the beautiful mountain town of Grand Lake Village, and drinking beer at the Lariat Saloon, Jet-Skiing on the lake, hiking up to Adams Falls, eating dinner at the Grand Lake Lodge, and shopping! Hello! Focus, girl.

I mentally slap my face. Then I mentally shrug my shoulders. Shopping is good therapy, and it's obvious Catherine needs good therapy. Especially with her two best friends.

My sister, Rachel, is two years older and two inches taller than I am. The main difference between the two of us is she wears her nails natural and she has about a gazillion more bucks than I do. She and her husband, Sam Bootie, are the bagel king and queen of Boulder. "Bootie's Bagels—the best in Boulder" are everywhere

23

now, especially since they franchised a few years ago. It's nice having royalty in the family. With it come fringe benefits, like a four-million-dollar vacation home in Grand Lake Village. And the nice thing is they share.

Catherine smiles and I can see the relief in her eyes.

"Oh wow! That'd be great. Cynthia, can you clear your schedule?"

"Of course! Dave's working in Europe for the next two weeks, and I can always pass my clients over to the new girls in the salon."

Good thing Cynthia owns the salon. Doing hair and nails is more of a hobby for her than a full-time job.

When can we leave?" Catherine asks.

"No better time than the present," I tell her. "You can drop your car off at my place, and then I'll drive you over to your condo so you can get your stuff and call your boss. Then I'll call Amiga's and tell them I have to take the next two weeks off. You can spend the night with me, and we'll drive up first thing in the morning. How does that sound?"

"Perfect!"

"I'll need to call and reschedule my clients tomorrow," Cynthia tells us. "That may take me some time, so I better drive up on my own. I should be able to get there by noon. Can we meet somewhere in town before we boat over to the house?"

"We can meet at Pancho & Lefty's for lunch," I tell her. "It's on the main drag, and I'll give you directions. That way we can leave our cars at the yacht club next door, where Rachel and Sam have several boats docked. I have a Moomba up there, a ski boat for my kids, and we can use that. Sam has a pontoon and an antique Chris-Craft, but I've never driven them. They both scare me."

"Why would the boats scare you?" Catherine asks me suspiciously.

"The pontoon is too big and the Chris-Craft is insanely expensive."

Catherine nods her head. "Okay, just checking. I thought maybe you've had some premonitions about them. I don't want to get in any boats with bad juju."

"Grand Lake has a yacht club?" Cynthia asks in surprise. "I didn't think the lake was big enough for yachts."

"Well, no, it's not. And there are no yachts up there, but Grand Lake has always had a yacht club. It's a local society thing, what can I tell you?"

"Oh, I'm starting to relax already," Catherine tells us. "And now I need a good cup of coffee. Shall I order some for us?"

A few minutes later the waiter comes up and places a large carafe at Catherine's elbow. "I'll pour, ladies, then we can toast to our trip to Grand Lake."

Catherine fills our cups, we do our toast, and I start sipping the bold French roast coffee we all love while I look around the patio.

Then I see him.

The man in my vision.

I swallow hard and sit up.

"Don't move," I warn Catherine and lean forward so she and Cynthia can hear my whisper. "Act natural and don't jump up when I tell you this, but I think I see that Dusty guy. He's sitting right behind you."

"Act natural?" Catherine squeaks in a high-pitched voice. "How can I act natural when a dyslexic mobster might be pulling a gun out and whacking me any second?"

"Don't panic. I don't see a gun anywhere. He's eating a big sandwich, so he has his hands full. I'm positive he's the guy I saw in my vision."

I pull out my lip gloss and apply it liberally. Actually, I think I missed my lips altogether, but I don't think anyone's noticed. I try to appear relaxed because I don't want Dusty to know we know he's sitting behind us. And yeah, missing my lips makes me look *so* relaxed.

"I've got a plan," I tell my friends. "I'll divert his attention, and Cynthia, you grab Catherine and run for cover. Go to your place and I'll meet you there."

"What are you going to do?" Catherine asks nervously.

Then she gets a look on her face like a lightbulb went off in her brain, or she discovered the molecular composition of fat DNA or something, and reaches an arm out to me. "Wait, Constance!"

Too late. I grab the silver carafe of coffee and throw it hard. "Run, Catherine!" I yell.

The carafe smacks the guy right in the forehead. Coffee flies everywhere as he groans and keels over on the patio floor.

Several patrons scream, and wait staff run out to the patio.

"Oh God! You hit my bodyguard," Catherine wails.

"Wait a minute! You have a bodyguard?" I squeal in disbelief. "Since when, and why didn't you tell me? Did I kill him?"

We run over to the huge black man lying on the ground. The guy moans and shakes his head. Cynthia, Catherine, and I grab his arms to help him sit up. We grunt and struggle, but he slips out of our grasp, and the back of his head hits the cement patio. He stares up at us with dazed eyes.

"Oh jeez, I'm sorry," I cry. "I thought he was Dusty."

"No, his name is Samson, and Jack hired him this afternoon to watch over me until all this mess is over," says Catherine.

Samson glares up at me. "Dusty? For God's sake, lady! Do I look Italian?"

He tries to sit up, but wobbles and loses his balance. He falls back and hits the other side of his head.

"Well, excuse me!" I'm indignant. "I thought there were black men in every country. There are black Englishmen, black Germans, black Frenchmen, black Russians...or, wait. Is that a drink?"

"We've got to get him to an emergency room," Catherine cries out. "He may have a concussion…or two."

Samson manages to sit up and grabs his head. "No shit! And third-degree burns," he croaks. "Call an ambulance and get me out of this hell. You don't need protection from the mob, lady. They need protection from you!"

Then Samson's eyes roll back into his head and he passes out.

SIX

Dusty Galucci is sitting on the patio of the Red Robin Restaurant across from Gordon Biersch watching the EMTs struggle to put a large black man onto a stretcher.

He giggles to himself, causing several patrons sitting nearby to look his way with concern and then discreetly inch their chairs away from him.

But Dusty isn't paying attention to anything but the commotion at Gordon's.

This is going to be so easy, Dusty thinks to himself. *Those dingy broads don't even know I'm watching them right now, and I could whack them anytime. All I have to do is watch those bimbos until the right time and then—POW! Shit, my uncle is gonna to be so proud of me.*

A shadow crosses over Dusty's face. He looks up and blinks when he sees his uncle standing over him.

"Uncle Rocky, what'cha doing here?" Dusty squirms under his uncle's scrutinizing glare.

Rocky Galucci was once a good-looking Italian hunk. Probably that was fifty years ago. Today he's a cross between Tony Soprano and Danny Devito. But even with his thinning hair and big belly, power and self-confidence emanate from his every pore.

When Rocky talked, people listened. When he snapped his fingers, people jumped.

When his dead brown eyes glared, people whimpered.

Everyone, that is, except his wife of forty years, Rosalina. Rosalina is short and squatty, and she didn't take shit off nobody. She had two hundred years of mafioso lineage running through her veins, and maybe when Rocky talked, people listened, but when *Rosalina* grunted, people stood at attention. The two of them together were a force to contend with.

Rocky slaps his nephew on the side of his head—a typical Italian gesture of disgust.

"I've been lookin' for ya, dirt wad. You didn't answer your cell phone. How ya gonna help the family if we can't get in touch with you? What'd ya doin' here?"

"I'm tailin' my mark. That's the James broad over there at Gordon's with the two blondes. They just clocked that black dude on the head with a coffeepot. I'm followin' her so I can establish her pattern and know whens a good time to whack her."

"Establish her pattern? That's some real sophisticated talkin' you're saying there, dirt wad. I just hope ya know what you're doin'."

Dusty feels a pang of fear in the pit of his stomach. He works hard to keep the tremble out of his voice, and makes sure his question comes across respectful.

"How'd ya find me? And my street name is Dusty, Uncle. Not dirt wad."

"Dusty, dirt wad, same difference to me. I gotta GPS chip in your cell phone, that's how I found ya. I got 'em in everyone's cell."

Rocky hesitates a second. "Except for Rosalina's. That woman would string me up by my balls if she found one in her cell."

Both men began nodding their heads in agreement. Then Dusty jerks to a stop when he realizes that maybe agreeing with his uncle isn't such a good idea. It's one thing to know how much power Rosalina has over Rocky, but it's another to acknowledge it in front of his uncle.

Fortunately, Rocky isn't watching him. He's watching the activity at Gordon's.

Rocky's cell beeps and he grabs it out of his coat pocket and looks at the caller ID.

"I gotta take this, but make sure you get this job done fast. And for Chrissake, go home, take a bath, and put on some clean clothes. Ya look like one of them street people."

Rocky starts to leave but stops and turns around with an evil smile. "Oh, and by the way, your mark left the restaurant with her two friends about five minutes ago. You better get off your ass and find her so ya can keep 'establishing' her pattern."

Rocky's wicked laughter rings in Dusty's ears as he darts across to Gordon's.

SEVEN

Catherine, Cynthia, and I are sitting in Poncho and Lefty's Mexican Restaurant in Grand Lake Village the next afternoon. Big burritos are in front of us.

"What do you mean, do we know what to do?" I'm addressing Cynthia's question to us.

"I mean," Cynthia says patiently, "what do any of us know about stopping a hit man?"

Good question.

"Look at us," Cynthia continues. "Constance, you were in finance all your life and a CFO until you retired. Catherine, you're a writer, and I'm a hairstylist and nail tech. Have any of you had any training in judo, karate, or self-defense? How do we stop this Dusty guy?"

We all look thoughtful.

"My three grandchildren take karate lessons," I say.

"I've seen *Home Alone* at least four times," Cynthia offers.

"I raised five kids, so I know a lot of survival skills," Catherine tells us.

Cynthia sighs. "So, what do we do if he finds us? Right now all we've got is Constance checking out his financials and helping him accessorize his outfit, Catherine teaching him proper grammar, and me cutting his hair and giving him a French manicure. I'm sure he's shaking in his shoes thinking about all the bad things we could do to him. Let's face it. We're toast unless we come up with a plan to protect Catherine."

We all sigh in unison.

"I didn't think about him finding us," I say. "I figured all we had to do was skip town and hide out for a few weeks until all this blows over. Do you think he followed us up here?"

The three of us slowly look around the room. Besides us, the only other people in the restaurant are a family with three kids under the age of five.

"We know he's not in this place, but if he didn't follow us up, he could probably use some of his 'family' connections to find out where we're staying," I say. "Problem is, we don't know what he looks like. Catherine, do you think your boss could fax us a picture of him?"

"That's a good idea. I'll give him a call when we get to your sister's house. I'm sure he can get us one."

"Why don't we hurry up and eat so we can get over to the house," I tell the others. "We may need to come back and get some things at the grocery store before it gets too dark."

Half an hour later, we're on the wood sidewalk outside of Poncho and Lefty's with about two thousand people. It's Wednesday and the tourists and those with vacation homes are coming in for the weekend.

"Holy smoley," Cynthia exclaims. "It wasn't this crowded when we got here."

"Oh, just wait, girlfriend," I tell her. "By tomorrow night this place will be packed. And next week is July Fourth, so you ain't seen nothing yet. This place will be wall-to-wall people. But it's fun. They'll have sailboat regattas and a parade, a flyover by the Air Force Academy, and fireworks over the lake."

We walk over to the yacht club marina, and I pick up the keys to my Moomba. When we get to the boat, we realize we have a problem.

The Moomba is a speedboat that seats four to five, and has absolutely no luggage space.

We're standing on the dock with our six big suitcases and numerous other travel bags, staring at the beautiful blue boat.

"Does the yacht club offer valet service?" Catherine asks.

"Good time to find out," I answer her.

EIGHT

An hour later I'm docking the Moomba at my sister's house. Catherine and Cynthia are behind me, riding with Rick, the Grand Lake tour guide, in his big pontoon.

I jump out of my boat and tie her up to the lakeside dock. Later I'll open the water garage attached to the house and lock the Moomba up for the night.

The pontoon pulls up and I grab a line and tie it up to the dock. Catherine and Cynthia get out, and Rick hands our suitcases over to us.

"Thanks, Rick," I holler to him when we have our luggage and he's ready to take off.

"Be sure to bring your lady friends over for a tour of Grand Lake," he hollers at me. "And call me when you need help getting everything back to the marina."

"I will," I assure him as I untie his boat. "Because all this luggage would sink my Moomba."

Rick grins and then backs the pontoon away from the dock, and in seconds he's flying through the dark waters across the lake.

I turn and see Catherine and Cynthia looking at the house with their mouths wide open.

It is impressive.

"Ladies," I tell them as I come up and put my arms through theirs. "Welcome to Bootie's Hideaway. Ten thousand square feet of brick, stone, mortar, and pine nestled against the southern shore of Grand Lake with the most magnificent view of Mount Baldy."

"Holy monkey balls," Cynthia exclaims. "How many bagels did it take to buy this place?"

"Probably about a billion," I tell her.

"That's a heck of a lot of bagels."

"Well, let's get everything in, and I'll give you the grand tour."

We drag our stuff across the manicured lawn and polished slate patio scattered with custom-made pine furniture to the front door. I enter the code and we pull our suitcases inside.

If the outside is impressive, the inside is incredible.

I show Catherine and Cynthia through the entire three stories, and after much oohing and aahing, we end up on the main level on the outside wraparound porch.

"Well, ladies, there are six bedrooms with attached baths upstairs, so grab your bags and pick one," I tell them.

We all tromp back inside and collect our bags.

"Can we stick close together?" Catherine asks.

"Good idea. Let's take either the three bedrooms facing the lake with the balconies, or the ones on the other side with the view of the mountain and the connecting decks," I suggest.

"I vote for the mountain view." This is from Cynthia. "That way if Dusty comes lurking around in a boat, he won't see us out on the balconies."

"Good point," Catherine agrees. "But isn't there a trail behind the house?"

"Yes, but it's back quite a ways," I tell them. "You saw how the house backs up to the side of the mountain. There's nothing out there but trees, wilderness, and mountain critters, and it slopes up. You can't see the house from the trail."

"How far does that trail go?" Catherine asks.

"It's a rugged little trail that connects the east side of the lake to the west. I'll show you tomorrow in the Moomba. And speaking of the Moomba, let's unpack and then check out the kitchen to see if we need anything in town before it gets dark."

We each pick a room and quickly unpack.

Minutes later we're back down in the kitchen looking through the cabinets and Sub-Zero fridge.

Catherine whistles softly. "I think this is a fully stocked kitchen."

"Pretty much," I tell her. "Rachel and Sam have a couple that come over to clean once a week and keep things stocked up during the summer. I'm sure she called them this morning and told them we were coming. But I better check the bar to make sure we have all we need for our martinis."

"The fridge has everything a poor soul would need for roughing it in the Rockies," Cynthia tells us. "Tons of fresh fruits, veggies, milk, gourmet coffee, cream, luncheon meats, bread—you name it and it's here. And the freezer is full of steaks and fish and these little hard, rock-looking things."

I peek over her shoulder. "Those are frozen mini-bagels."

"Wow! Half the freezer is full of them."

"Yeah, Rachel loves mini-bagels, so she makes sure they have plenty up here."

I quickly check out the bar and see it's fully stocked too. "I think we've got everything we need here, so let's go to the office and you can call your boss on the landline, Catherine. We need to get a picture of Dusty faxed over, if he has one."

We tromp through the den, past the master bedroom suite to the office in back.

"Good grief! This place is filled with tons of neat stuff and a lot of opulence for a little getaway," Cynthia observes.

I look at her with surprise. "Oh, you must've seen the mirror over the bed in the master suite,"

"No," she gasps. "I was talking about that huge hot tub outside those French doors on that super-duper deck. But I'm going to check out the mirror now."

We run back to the master suite while Catherine makes her call.

"See?" I show her, pointing at the canopy over the enormous four-poster pine bed in the middle of the room.

"Oh my God," Cynthia exclaims. Then she squints her eyes and looks closer. "There are cute little bare bottoms on each corner."

"Actually, those are caricatures of Sam's butt."

"Shut the back door! You've got to be kidding me."

We both fall back onto the bed and stare up at the mirror in amazement.

Then we start giggling, which opens the floodgates, and before we know it we're laughing hysterically. Probably the butts on the mirror aren't all that funny, but the laughter releases the pent-up anxiety we've been holding in for the past two days, and we can't help ourselves. We snort and gasp as we try to help each other sit up.

Catherine rushes into the room. "What's going on?"

Cynthia and I fall back on the bed, and I point to the mirror, wiping the tears from my cheeks.

"We're looking at the caricatures of Sam's butt on the mirror over their bed," I tell her.

Catherine lies down between us and starts giggling immediately.

"Oh Lord. Did he pose for those?" she asks me.

"I don't know. All I know is Rachel had this custom-made and installed for Sam's sixtieth birthday several years ago as a surprise. Rachel told me Sam was voted as having the cutest butt in high school and college. And with a last name of Bootie, it became a big joke. Rachel's always teasing him about it and is thinking of making this caricature into a family crest—Sam's personal coat of arms."

"You mean, his personal coat of butts," Catherine blurts out.

"I bet Bootie's Bagels has a lot of great *assets*! And a terrific *bottom* line." That's from Cynthia.

"Oh, we've got to quit making him the *butt* of our jokes," I howl.

For the next five minutes, we lie on the bed looking up at the mirror and laughing our heads off.

NINE

When we finally get ourselves under control, we venture back to the den. Since we don't have to go back into town, I go out and pull my Moomba into the water garage while Cynthia makes three Lemon Drop Martinis.

Then we sit on the front porch overlooking the lake while we watch the sunset and sip our martinis.

"I took three steaks out of the freezer when we got here," Catherine tells us. "We can grill those, fix a nice salad, and there's some fresh Asiago cheese bread in the fridge to go along with it."

"Were you able to get in touch with Jack?" I ask Catherine.

"Yes, but he doesn't have a picture of Dusty, so he's going to contact the police tomorrow and see if he can get one to fax to us."

"Did he give you a report on Samson?" Cynthia asks. "I sure hope he's okay, and doesn't decide to sue us or the paper."

"I sent him flowers this morning before we left," Catherine tells me. "And Jack told me the paper is taking care of all his medical bills and paying him while he recovers. He has a mild concussion, but he's going to be okay. I think in his profession, getting roughed up is part of the norm."

"Yeah, but not from three flaky females," I retort. "I feel so bad about whacking him on the head with that carafe, but I had no idea he was there to protect you, Catherine."

"I should've told you about him, but I forgot he was there, to be truthful with you. I'm not used to having a bodyguard following me around."

"So much for the accuracy of my premonitions," I tell my friends.

"Hey, it's not your fault, Constance," Catherine says. "You've had those for years and they've always been a little unpredictable."

"You know what, guys," Cynthia pipes in. "While we were walking downtown today, I saw an ad on one of those community bulletin boards about a psychic who lives in Granby, and I wrote down her phone number. Maybe we could make an appointment and drive over to see her. She might be able to help us. Maybe even foresee what's going to happen in the future so we can be prepared."

"Sure wouldn't hurt," I agree.

"I'll go call her right now. We might not be able to get appointments right away." Cynthia gets up and goes into the house.

A few minutes later she comes back with a big smile on her face.

"You won't believe this, but she has an opening tomorrow morning. How cool is that?"

I groan. "I hope she's not a flake or a fake."

Cynthia picks up her martini and stares at me. "Don't be such a cynic. I'm surprised you said that, with all the paranormal experiences you have."

"You're right, and I apologize."

"Besides," Cynthia says with a grin, "we can test her. I didn't tell her you have premonitions, so let's see if she picks up on that tomorrow when we meet. If she's the real thing, she should recognize someone with paranormal abilities. If she's a fake, she won't and all she'll do is give us a big song and dance."

"Yeah," says Catherine, "and charge us an arm and leg while she's doing it."

TEN

At ten o'clock the next morning, we're in the Moomba heading for Grand Lake Village. It's a beautiful, sunny day, and the lake is as smooth as glass.

When we get to the marina, we tie up the Moomba and spend a few minutes strolling up and down Grand Avenue looking at the shops. The crowds are quickly growing, so we head back to the marina and pick up Cynthia's Mercedes for our short trip to Granby.

"I sure hope this woman is the real thing," I tell my two friends when we get in the car. "What's her name?"

Cynthia pulls a paper out of her purse and looks at it. "Flavia Foret," she tells us.

I can't help myself. I know my eyebrows are raised as high as the ceiling in Cynthia's car.

"Flavia? We're going to see someone named Flavia? What kind of name is Flavia?"

"A very unusual one, I agree. But let's not get any preconceived ideas until we meet her. After all, we still don't know what this Dusty guy looks like and we need all the help we can get."

"You're right, I know. I guess I'm nervous about everything that's going on, and I've never been to a psychic or fortune-teller before."

"It doesn't hurt to try new things. If nothing else we'll enjoy a beautiful drive to

Granby, and then when we're done, we can have lunch when we get back to Grand Lake Village."

"Oh, you're right. And after lunch we can do some shopping in town, and then we'll take the Moomba out. I'll show you Rainbow Bridge, and we'll boat around Shadow Mountain Lake and Grand Lake. It's a gorgeous day and hopefully we left Dusty in the dust back in Denver. Let's enjoy ourselves."

The drive to Granby is fun. Cynthia puts in an Abba CD and soon we're singing to "Dancing Queen" at the top of our lungs.

When we get to Granby, we find Flavia's house a few blocks off the main highway. I'm a little surprised when we pull up to a modest, cookie-cutter house in the suburbs.

"Wow! This is such a normal house. I was expecting something, you know, much more flamboyant, and Hollywood."

"Right, like something Whoopi Goldberg would come strolling out of from that movie, *Ghost*," Catherine says. "A house painted a psychedelic green, pink, and purple, with beads and heavy curtains hanging from the windows."

The three of us walk up to the front door, and before we can knock, it opens.

"Come in, come in. I've been expecting you."

The young lady at the door is one of the most beautiful women I've ever seen. She's in her late twenties or early thirties, with long dark hair, dark eyes, dark complexion, and a gorgeous slender body. And I would've killed for her outfit—flowing black skirt, tight white gauzy top with dozens of necklaces, and both arms covered with brilliant bangles from her wrists to her elbows.

The three of us freeze.

The lady flashes a brilliant smile and immediately grabs Catherine's hand and pulls her in the house. Cynthia and I follow.

"I'm Flavia. Please, come in."

Flavia's voice has a soft accent I can't identify. But it's soothing and mesmerizing.

Flavia looks at each of us with her piercing black eyes. When she comes to me, she stops and her eyes widen.

"You!" she says with surprise. "You have paranormal powers. I can feel them, and I can see them in your aura."

"You can see auras?" I ask in a stunned voice.

"Yes, and yours is dazzling and strong. Oh, I'm sorry. I don't mean to frighten or disturb you. It's just that I don't see auras like yours very often. In fact, they're rare. But you're all here for a reason, so why don't you come in and relax and please, sit down. You're a very unusual group. I'm sensing some strong vibes from all of you."

That's us. The three Chiquititas with strong vibes.

We sit down in her comfortable and brightly decorated living room. A small Russell Terrier dog comes in and sits at Flavia's feet.

Okay. That does it. I'm completely blown away.

First, Flavia knows I have paranormal powers just by looking at me.

Second, she's beautiful, a trendy dresser, and doesn't look a *thing* like Whoopi.

And third, well, she has a *freakin'* dog. If anything I'd expect her to have a black cat. But, noooo. My psychic lives with her little Skippy dog in a modest, suburban home.

Frankly, I think she's a disgrace to the psychic profession and has completely tarnished my image of fortune-tellers forever.

ELEVEN

We sit looking at Flavia, and she's sitting across the room looking at us.

"Would you like to do a group session, or separate sessions?" she asks us.

We look at one another and then back at her. So far all we've been able to do since we arrive is stare at her and one another.

I clear my throat. "We're not sure," I tell her. "Personally, I've never been to a psychic or fortune-teller before, so I don't know what to expect."

I turn to my friends. "What about you two? Have you ever been to a psychic before?"

Catherine and Cynthia shake their heads no.

I look at Flavia. "Why don't we start with a group session?"

Flavia leans back in her overstuffed chair and studies us a minute. Then she leans forward and clasps her hands together.
"Okay, first let me tell you about the strong vibes I'm feeling." She looks at Catherine. "You, dear lady, are in some kind of trouble, am I right?"

Catherine nods.

"And you." She's looking at me now. "You have paranormal abilities but you've never been trained to control them, or explore what other gifts you might have. Probably because you just accepted what you had and never delved any deeper into the paranormal, or had anyone to mentor you."

I nod.

Now she looks at Cynthia. "Hmmm, interesting. I think you're the glue that holds this group together."

I clear my throat. "You're good. Would you like for us to tell you our names, or do you already know them? I mean, I'm not being disrespectful, but you've kinda surprised us with your accuracy so far."

Flavia smiles. "I'm a true psychic, not a fake, but no, I don't know your names, and I apologize for my lack of manners. I'm not usually hit with so much so fast. Please." She gestures with her hands. "Introduce yourselves."

"My name is Constance, and the one in trouble is Catherine, and Cynthia is the one with the glue." Which makes sense to me, because Cynthia uses a lot of nail glue in her line of work.

Flavia looks us over. "Okay, now please, tell me why you're here."

"It's because of me," Catherine tells her. "I'm a syndicated columnist for the *Denver Advocate*, and I wrote an expose on the mob connections with the Columbia drug cartel that came out in last Sunday's paper. The mob killed my informant, and they put a contract out on me. These are my two best friends, and we came up to Grand Lake Village to hide out until everything blows over."

"And I started having premonitions when I was seven, and I saw a premonition of

Catherine and knew she was in danger," I tell her.

Cynthia shrugs. "I just highlight their hair and do their nails."

"We're hoping you can foresee our future, or at least Catherine's, and tell us what we should do to keep her safe and away from the guy who's trying to whack her," I confess.

Flavia doesn't say anything for a full minute. She looks at each of us carefully.

"Let me do a quick reading on Catherine. Maybe I can see if there's any danger in her immediate future."

Flavia walks over to Catherine, kneels down, and gently takes her hands. She closes her eyes and everything is silent for several minutes.

Cynthia, Catherine, and I peek at one another. I don't know about them, but I'm expecting Flavia to go into some sort of trance and start speaking fluent mumbo jumbo any second now.

But all we get is silence.

Finally Flavia opens her eyes and looks at Catherine.

"I sense some present danger, but then it oddly dissipates. Let me read Constance since she has the paranormal abilities."

She walks to me and takes my hands. The second her fingers touch mine, a sharp sizzle rips through my body. I cry out and Flavia gasps, drops my hands, and jumps back. Her eyes are wide with shock. Mine are even wider.

"*Mon Dieu!*" she exclaims.

And *now* the mumbo jumbo starts.

I don't know about the other two Chiquititas, but my feet are heading for the front door.

"Stop! Please stop," Flavia shouts. "It's okay, really. I need to explain."

The three of us stop, but only because we can't all fit through the front door at the same time.

"What was that all about?" I demand, turning around and facing her. "That hurt."

"Oh, I'm so sorry," Flavia wailed. "I was trying to use my telepathic energy to infiltrate yours, and it caused a rare psychic phenomenon. It's like a static electric shock, only worse."

"No shit it's worse! I'm lucky I didn't pee my pants." I wiggle back and forth on my feet. "And I'm not so sure I didn't."

I see the worry in Flavia's eyes and stop and sigh.

"Alright. I'll stay, but please don't touch me like that again."

"No, I promise. I won't."

We all walk back into her living room and sit down.

"First, what was that mumbo jumbo you were speaking when this happened?" I ask her.

Flavia smiles. "That was Cajun French. Sometimes I revert back to my native tongue when I'm upset or startled. I was born and raised in the small town of Dulac, south of New Orleans."

"Ah. I wondered where you were from when I heard your accent."

51

"I moved here two years ago with my boyfriend. It's been...challenging. I think I'm over the culture shock now, and I love the mountains. But it's taken the townsfolk a little time to accept me, especially since I'm a psychic."

She sighs. "Ladies, I need to do some research and consult with someone before we go any further. I'd like to do tarot card readings with each of you, but not today. I'm afraid that little zap Constance and I experienced drained my psychic power. Can you come back on Monday? I think I'll be ready by then. But I need to warn you. Things may not turn out like you think. And you may not appreciate all you learn or hear from me. Can you handle that?"

The three of us look at one another, and then back at Flavia. We all nod our heads yes.

And that's when I have another premonition.

TWELVE

In the haze of my premonition, I see an older man about my age with a Roman nose. Definitely Italian. He has thick, wavy, black hair that's gray around the temples, and muscles. He gets off a big Harley-Davidson motorcycle in front of Poncho and Lefty's. He pulls off his sunglasses and looks around, and then walks toward the marina.

My premonition ends, and I fall back on Flavia's living room couch.

"Oh no! I saw Dusty! And he's coming to Grand Lake Village."

Flavia runs over and takes my hand. "What did you see?"

"I saw an Italian man get off a motorcycle in front of Poncho and Lefty's and walk toward the marina. I think it's the guy who's trying to whack Catherine."

"Did you see anything else?"

"No. My premonitions are never long. But I did get a good look at his face." I look over at Constance and Cynthia. "I know I'd recognize him again. I'm sure of it."

Everyone is leaning over me. Flavia is gently rubbing my hand and murmuring under her breath.

I sit up straight.

"Oh. My. God! What are we going to do? We've got to get back to Grand Lake. Do you think he knows where we're staying? He probably has a picture of Catherine. Oh, crap!

He may have pictures of all of us. He may be waiting for us at the marina. Do you think he knows which boat is mine? How do we avoid him?"

I'm hyperventilating and close to an all-out panic attack.

"Calm down," Flavia tells me. "Now that you know what he looks like, you can turn the tables. Instead of running away, you can follow him, find out where he's staying, what he's up to. Don't you see? You can protect yourselves by being the stalkers."

Flavia looks us over. "But first, I think you need some disguises in case he does have photos. I have a ton of costumes I use when I'm hired to give fortunes at special events and parties. You wouldn't believe what people expect fortune tellers to wear—turbans and hats and all sorts of wild Gypsy clothing."

I roll my eyes like I can't believe it either and I would *never* think such a thing when I know that's exactly what I was thinking. I'm such a hypocrite.

"I even have wigs," she continues. "Let me dig out some things, and let's see what we can come up with."

She runs out and a few minutes later, she brings a large box in the room. "Start looking through this and I'll bring you more stuff."

Thirty minutes later the three of us leave Flavia's house totally incognito.

Catherine has on a slinky black jumpsuit with a big silver belt, a long dark wig covered by a floppy black sun hat, huge oversized sunglasses, and silver stilettos.

Cynthia is wearing a turban tied around her spray-painted blue hair, John Lennon sunglasses, a shirt tied around her midriff, flared flower pants, and Jesus sandals.

I'm wearing a pink wig with short, pointy spikes that could be considered lethal weapons, skin-tight neon-yellow capri pants, a sheer blouse over a tank top, big white-framed sunglasses, and five-inch white platform heels.

Here we are. Posh, Katy Perry, and Lady Gaga.

And it's not even Halloween.

THIRTEEN

"I don't know about you two," I tell my friends, "but I feel ridiculous in this outfit. And I can't walk in these dang platform heels."

We're back in Grand Lake Village walking down Grand Avenue, heading toward the Sagebrush Café for lunch.

"I feel like everyone is staring at us. I'm afraid we stand out in these costumes."

"Seriously?" Cynthia turns and looks at me. "Seriously, Constance? Look around you." She waves her arms. "This place is crawling with tourists, and most of them look crazier than we do."

I stop and watch two guys saunter past us. One has a tricolor Mohawk in black, yellow, and red. His pants are falling down his butt, and he has piercings and tattoos on every inch of his exposed skinny body. The other is dressed in black leather pants and chaps, with a matching vest that barely fits around his bulging bare chest. The sun bounces off his bald head, but it's the large silver hoop earrings in both ears that catch the rays and almost blind me.

I nearly run into a happy tourist wearing tan shorts and matching T-shirt who would've looked halfway normal if he hadn't been wearing black nylon socks pulled up to his knobby knees and black dress shoes. He's the male equivalent to Maxine.

Cynthia's right. Grand Lake is swarming with weirdos.

And we fit right in there with them.

"Point taken," I tell her.

We get to the Sagebrush Café, and after a ten-minute wait we finally sit down and order buffalo burgers and beer.

We're eating peanuts and throwing the shells on the old wood floor when I look up and see Dusty across the restaurant. The Sagebrush has rooms on the second floor above the café, and he's standing by the check-in counter with his back to us, obviously waiting for a room key.

"Omigod!" I gasp. "There's Dusty."

"Where?" asks Catherine in alarm.

"Right behind you getting a room key."

Catherine and Cynthia turn and stare.

"I dunno if that's him," Catherine says with a frown. "Jack told me on the phone yesterday that Dusty is a small, mousy-looking guy, in his thirties, with receding hair. That man doesn't look anything like the guy Jack described."

"But that's the man I saw in my vision. Do you suppose the mob sent someone else to whack you?" I ask. "Maybe they decided to give up on Dusty."

"Could be," Catherine says thoughtfully. "But how do we find out?"

"One of us should follow him and see which room he goes into," says Cynthia. "He's probably going to drop his stuff off and come right back out to look for Catherine. When he does, we can sneak up there and see if we can find some identification."

"Are you serious?" I ask. "How are we going to break into his room? I've never picked a lock in my life. Have you? And I'm not even going to think about how illegal this is."

"Nope," Catherine shakes her head. "I've never picked a lock in my life either, but several years ago I dated a guy who kept locking himself out of his condo. He used a credit card to get in, and I think I remember how he did it."

"Maybe we'll find a name on a prescription bottle, or some credit card receipts," suggests Cynthia. "Men usually like to empty out their pockets when they check into a room. I know Dave does."

"What do you think we're going to find?" I ask them. "A luggage tag with his business card that says, 'Al Capone, Mob Hit Man—You Pay, I Slay'?" I shake my head in disbelief. "Okay, I can't believe we're even thinking about this, but how about this plan. Cynthia, since you're wearing sandals and can get around easier than me or Catherine, you follow him and find out what room he's in, then come back down and tell us. When he leaves, Catherine and I will go up and see if we can get in and you can stand guard."

"That'll work," Cynthia says. "Look! He's going upstairs now, and I'm right behind him. Agent Ninety-nine, ten-four and out."

She gets up and follows our guy up the steps. A few minutes later, she's back at the table.

"Room five," she tells us. "Boy! That was easy. I checked out the doors to the rooms while I was up there, and they don't look like they have anything but simple locks on them."

"Oooo, look at us! We're like Charlie's Angels!" Catherine exclaims. "This is so exciting."

I'm thinking we're more like the Golden Girls or the Three Stooges, but I don't want to bust Catherine's bubble.

Our burgers come, and while we're eating, our guy comes back down. And wouldn't you know our freakin' luck. He doesn't leave the cafe, but plops down in a booth close by.

FOURTEEN

A sleek, black Cadillac pulls up to the front of the newly restored Grand Lake Lodge, and Dusty Galucci climbs out from behind the wheel. He's dressed in a snazzy new suit, polished Italian loafers, and Gucci sunglasses, gifts from his mother after he told her about Uncle Rocky's comments. She even let him borrow her car, and made sure he had a fresh haircut and manicure before leaving Denver that morning.

He looks around while the bright summer sun shines on his partially bald head and then opens his trunk and pulls out a suitcase.

Dusty gazes at the scenery as he climbs the stairs and enters the restored lobby filled with antiques and memoirs of days gone by.

The fresh mountain air annoys the hell out of him. He doesn't get it. Why would anyone pay good money to stay in this joint? As far as he's concerned, the only good places in the mountains are the towns with casinos.

One of the staff checks him in, gives him a brief history of the lodge, and tells him about the amenities offered with the room. It's obvious Dusty has no interest in anything the man is telling him, so he quickly stops talking and leads Dusty to his room.

"As if I give a shit," Dusty snorts as he looks at all the old photos and selective memorabilia on his way to his room.

In a matter of minutes, Dusty is alone and snooping around his bedroom, wondering if there's anything of value he could stuff in his suitcase. Seeing nothing of interest, he sits down at the small desk by the bed and pulls a map out of his pocket his uncle gave him.

Stupid broads, Dusty thinks to himself. *How much easier could they make it for me? They hide out in a house on Grand Lake that has a fuckin' trail right behind it.*

That afternoon he's going to take a little hike and stake out the house. All he has to do is find a spot close enough to pick off the James broad, and then he's getting out of here.

Dusty pulls a Marlboro out of his pocket and lights it, smirking at the "No Smoking" sign in the room.

FIFTEEN

Our mystery man finishes his lunch as we anxiously watch. It's a good thing his back is to us so he doesn't know he's under our surveillance. He pays his tab and then leaves with a slight glance around the restaurant.

My breath catches when he looks our way, but he continues out the door without giving us a second glance. Thank God we're not as noticeable as I thought.

"Okay, I'm on his tail," Cynthia tells us. "We all have our cell phones, so if he looks like he's headed back in this direction, I'll give one of you a call. Otherwise, let me know when you leave his room."

"Ten-four, Agent Ninety-nine," I tell her.

She gives me a thumbs-up and leaves the restaurant. Catherine and I get up and nonchalantly head for the stairs. When we reach the second floor, we locate room five. Catherine takes out her credit card and slides it down the door as she gently turns the knob. Amazingly, the door swings open and we look at each other in shock.

"As Cynthia would say, holy monkey balls! Good job, MacGyver," I exclaim.

We go in and shut the door.

It's a small room with a double bed, rustic dresser, nightstand, and a window overlooking Grand Avenue. On the bed is an unopened backpack and duffel bag. I quickly head for the bags on the bed, and Catherine goes into the tiny bathroom. No receipts are on the nightstand or dresser, and no name tags are on the bags. I open both bags, but there's nothing in them except several pair of jeans, a few shirts, underwear, and socks. I can't find anything to help us identity our mystery man. Not even his name inked in his Hanes "tighty-whitey" briefs, size thirty-six. I zip up the bags at the same time I hear the toilet flush.

"What are you doing?" I whisper loudly as I rush to the bathroom door. "You can't use his bathroom."

"Why not?" Catherine asks as she comes out.

"We have to be careful, or he'll know someone has been in his room! We have to leave everything just like we found it, and we can't leave any fingerprints or butt DNA. Quick! Wipe down the toilet seat and I'll do the bags." My heart is pounding.

"Butt DNA? Is that even possible?"

"I don't know. Anything's possible. Remember, we're dealing with the Mafia here."

We take tissues and wipe down the bags, doorknobs, and toilet seat.

"There's nothing in the bathroom except for his shaving bag," Catherine tells me. "And all he has in it is toothpaste and a razor—no prescription bottle with his name on it."

"I couldn't find anything in his bags or on his dresser to identify him either."

63

We finish our wipe down and then quietly lock and close the door and rush down the stairs.

I call Cynthia when we're outside.

"How'd it go?" she asks when she answers.

"Not so good. We got in the room, but we couldn't find anything to identify our man. Where are you now?"

"I followed him to the marina. He bought a ticket for the next Grand Lake Tour, so I bought three tickets for us. You and Catherine better get down here fast. They're going to take off in about ten minutes."

"We're on our way." I hang up. "Cynthia's at the marina. Our guy is getting ready to take the Grand Lake tour, so she bought tickets for us too," I tell Catherine as we hurry toward the lake.

Minutes later I spot Cynthia lounging on one of the benches by Rick's Grand Lake tour boat.

"You're just in time," she tells us. "They're loading up now."

Rick's big pontoon is about half full, with a line of people waiting to board, and I'm hoping he doesn't recognize us in our disguises. If he does, he'll be questioning me and I don't want our guy to overhear anything.

"Try to avoid Rick," I tell my friends. "Hang back so we can board last."

Our mystery man is in no hurry to get on either and is scrutinizing the crowd.

64

"We need to keep to ourselves and act like we're discussing something important," I tell my friends.

"We are discussing something really important. Like, why are we getting on this boat?" asks Catherine.

"Flavia told us to stalk him and find out what he's up to, so that's why I bought the tickets," Cynthia answers. "He's probably trying to locate Bootie's Hideaway and that's why he's taking the tour."

"But is it safe for us to be on same boat with him?" Catherine asks.

While we're having this discussion, we move closer to the boat. Fortunately, Rick is back by the wheel and not paying any attention to us. Unfortunately, our guy is directly in front of us.

We shut up and quietly board behind him. We're looking for seats together when I turn and notice our guy staring straight at Catherine.

Fear grips my heart. He moves to the side of the boat, but he never takes his eyes off Catherine. Then I watch as he reaches inside his jacket.

My heart is beating so hard, I can barely stand it. Catherine and Cynthia are still looking for seats and not paying any attention to what he's doing. But I can see that he's slowly pulling something out of his pocket.

I almost pass out. Now I'm sure he's recognized Catherine and he's pulling out a gun to whack her.

I have to do something.

And I do.

I grab my purse and swing it with both arms, knocking him in the chest. He loses his balance and falls into the lake.

"Man with a gun," I screech.

Then all hell breaks loose.

Women are screaming, kids are crying, and Catherine, Cynthia, and I are hauling ass to get out of the boat.

I have to push several hefty men out of my way, but I'm right behind my two friends. In seconds the three of us are running down the plank onto the boardwalk straight to the Moomba.

SIXTEEN

We make it back to the house in record time and rush in and lock the door. I told Cynthia and Catherine all the details of what happened on the ride back, and now we're standing in the foyer, breathing hard.

"We're safe, we're safe," Catherine is panting.

"Holy shit, holy shit," Cynthia is gasping.

"I need a drink, I need a drink," I wheeze. "And I'm pouring shots right now."

I go to the bar and get a bottle of good tequila out with three shot glasses. My hands are shaking, but I manage to get most of the tequila in the glasses.

Cynthia and Catherine come up and we each grab a glass.

"Wait." Catherine stops us before we can gulp anything down. "We need to do a toast. Can we do my favorite?"

Cynthia and I nod, and we all three say together, "Here's to your liver, lover."

We start giggling. That was a toast Catherine's mom and dad always said to each other. And it was the one thing her mom remembered even when she was in late-stage Alzheimer's. It was a fond memory of Catherine's, and it always made us feel good to do it.

It feels good to say it now.

I don't pour any more shots because I have to put the Moomba in the water garage for the night, and I don't want to miss the door.

We move away from the bar and start removing our disguises. I take off my wig and throw it down on the sofa, then reach for my shoes. My feet are killing me.

"I'm going to wash this blue stuff out of my hair," Cynthia tells us and heads for the stairs.

"Oh my." Catherine is looking at her cell phone. "In all the excitement I missed a call from my boss. I better call him back." She wanders off toward the office.

I sink into the sofa and pull my shoes off. At least my hands have stopped shaking. I run my fingers through my hair and think about our day and close call.

Catherine walks back into the den with some papers in her hand.

"Oh. My. God," she exclaims softly.

"What?" After what we've been through today, I can't imagine what could make her face turn any whiter.

"Constance, look at this! I just got off the phone with my boss, and he faxed over a picture of Dusty. And a picture of my new bodyguard."

Catherine hands the papers to me.

I'm sure the first one is Dusty. He's thin, partially bald, with a big nose and hairy eyebrows. And his name is printed at the bottom of the picture.

But it's the second picture that makes me groan out loud.

"Oh no!" I put my hand over my mouth. I can't believe it.

It's a picture of our mystery guy.

"Mick Carelli? That's your new bodyguard? Why didn't Jack tell us yesterday he was sending another bodyguard to replace Samson?"

"He didn't do it until today. He found out through his police connections that Dusty might be on his way up here, so he decided to hire this Mick guy. Which may explain who these unknown calls are from on my phone." She sighs and sinks down on the couch beside me.

I close my eyes and moan. "Oh God. We don't even know if this Mick is okay. I may have hurt him…or, do you think he may have drowned?" I sit up quickly and look at Catherine with terror in my eyes.

"No, he didn't drown, Constance. I looked back once and could see him being pulled out of the lake. He may be in police custody after the riot we caused, but I don't think he's dead."

I breathe a little easier. "He probably has identification, so he'll be okay with the police. But I have a feeling he's gonna be pissed if he finds out I'm the one who knocked him out of the boat."

I look at Catherine and panic has replaced the terror in my eyes. "Do you think he's coming to the house? What did your boss tell you?"

"Jack told me Mick was trying to get in touch with me, so yes, I think he's going to want to come to the house. Maybe even stay here."

"Well then, we've got to get out of these clothes and look like our regular selves. And we've got to tell Cynthia what's going on and hide our disguises."

I jump up, grab Flavia's platform heels, and run for the stairs with Catherine right behind me.

An hour later Cynthia and Catherine are sitting outside on the patio waiting for me. I put the Moomba in the garage, and by the time I get back, there's a Lemon Drop Martini with my name on it.

"You need to loosen up, Constance," Cynthia tells me when she hands me my drink.

I sink into a soft chair and sigh, and we do our toast.

SEVENTEEN

For the first time today, I relax. Really, really relax. Lemon Drop Martini relax. It feels great. I close my eyes. I'm safe. We're all safe. Safe from crazy psychics and psycho hit men.

"Constance, I need to tell you something and please don't panic," Catherine says to me real soft. "While you were putting up the Moomba, Mick called and he's on his way over."

My eyes fly open and I sit up. Then I make myself sit back. "It's okay. We packed up our disguises, so he'll never know we were the ones in that boat. When he gets here, we'll pretend we've never seen him before in our lives. It's good. I'm good."

We sit and sip and think about what we want for dinner. We're discussing food when I hear a boat approaching and I know it's Mick.

"Okay, ladies. Here he comes. Best foot forward. I'd say break a leg, but with our luck, one of us would probably do it."

We watch as Mick brings his boat up to the dock, and then we all walk to the pier. I grab the line he throws and secure his boat. He jumps out and walks up to us. I notice his thick hair is slightly damp.

Catherine leans over and whispers in my ear. "I don't see a wedding band, girlfriend."

"He probably lost it in the lake," I whisper back.

We watch as he approaches Catherine.

71

"Ms. James?" he asks.

"Yes, that's me. Jack faxed over your picture, but do you mind showing me some ID?"

He pulls a wallet out of his back pocket and flips it open. We all lean forward and look at it, and I stifle a nervous giggle when I see how drenched it is.

"Your wallet's all wet. What happened?" Catherine asks with a poker face.

"Oh, I had a little incident at the marina. Some crazy lady thought I had a gun and knocked me into the water."

We look at him with sympathy. We are so bad.

"Everyone is so paranoid these days with all the random shootings going on, don't ya think?" Catherine shakes her head and tsks. "Do you carry a gun?"

"Sometimes, but I didn't have one on me when this happened. I was on the boat for the Grand Lake tour and reached in my pocket for my sunglasses. This nutty woman saw me and started yelling about a man with a gun and knocked me overboard with her purse."

"Wow, that must have been some purse," Catherine continues, and we look at him with big, innocent eyes.

We are so going to hell in a handbasket.

"Let me introduce you to my two best friends, Constance and Cynthia."

We shake hands and then we all nonchalantly stroll back to the patio.

"Would you like a drink?" I ask him. "We're having martinis, but we have beer, wine, and a fully stocked bar."

He's watching Catherine intently, but then he turns his eyes on me.

"Sure. A beer would be good."

"We've got Michelob, Stella, Coors, and Bud Light, cans or bottles."

He smiles and his whole countenance changes. Yowzer! He's not bad looking for a guy with a big, Roman nose.

"Do you have Coors in a bottle?"

"Sure thing. You want a glass?"

"No, bottle will be fine."

I escape to the house and breathe a sigh of relief. So far, so good. When I get back with the beer, everyone is sitting around the patio table chatting away like long-lost friends. I hear Catherine telling Mick about what's happened so far.

When she finishes, Mick turns his piercing brown eyes on me.

"So, this is your sister's house?"

"Yes, my sister and brother-in-law are Sam and Rachel Bootie. They bought this place several years ago. Since it's off the beaten path and difficult to get to, I thought it'd be the perfect place for Catherine to hide out. Plus, it has a state-of-the-art security system."

"Can you get to it from the back?" he asks.

"You can, but there's a lot of dense underbrush and woods from the trail to the house."

"I need to check out the house and property if you don't mind."

"Sure. Let me show you through the house, and then you can wander around all you want."

"Catherine and I will check the fridge and freezer and find something for dinner while you're doing that," Cynthia says. "What are your plans, Mr. Carelli? Are you going to camp out here with us?"

"I think it's better if I do. I've got a room at the Sagebrush, but I'll call them and check out over the phone. I brought all my stuff with me when I rented the boat to come over. And everyone, please, call me Mick."

"Okay, Mick," I tell him. "You can stay in either the master bedroom downstairs, or in one of the bedrooms upstairs. Let me give you the tour."

He grabs the backpack and duffel bag I searched a few hours earlier and drops them in the foyer. I hide my smile as I think about the "tighty-whities" packed in his bag. I'm such a pervert. I show him around the house and we end up in the kitchen with Catherine and Cynthia.

"I think I'll check around outside before I take my bags upstairs," he tells us and slips through one of the back patio doors.

"Mick decided to bunk out in the middle bedroom across from you, Catherine," I say. "He didn't seem too interested in sleeping under Sam's mirror in the master suite downstairs."

"What a relief he didn't recognize us. I think we dodged a bullet, no pun intended," Cynthia says while looking through the freezer. "How about some grilled salmon fillets tonight?"

"Sounds good to me. With rice and a green salad?" I ask them.

"Oh, yeah," Catherine agrees. "And maybe some garlic bread."

I put an Adele CD in the sound system and we continue with our dinner prep while we chat about our day. In a few minutes Mick comes back in, and we can hear him in the den coming toward the kitchen.

"I checked the backyard," he hollers to us. "It's thick with foliage and undergrowth, but it doesn't look like anyone's been back there, or…"

Mick stops talking and we look at one another. A minute later he walks in the kitchen. He's holding my pink Lady Gaga wig out with two fingers, and the three of us freeze. His brown eyes penetrate my blue ones and I can tell he's pissed.

"Lucy," he says to me, holding up the wig. "You've got some 'splaining to do."

EIGHTEEN

"How do you know that's mine?" I ask him. My eyes are as big as saucers.

"You're the one who knocked my partner out the other night, so I knew it had to be yours. You fit the profile." He slowly reaches in his shirt pocket and pulls out some pink tufts that match the wig. "And you were in my room this afternoon too, weren't you?"

"Oh, shit," I mumble softly. I throw up my hands and walk to the dining room and plop down in a chair. "I don't believe this! We were so careful not to leave any fingerprints or butt DNA in the room, and then my stupid wig sheds and gives us away. Okay, okay, sit down, Mr. Carelli, and I'll explain everything."

"I'll get you another beer, Mick," Cynthia offers. "You'll need it. And then we'll all sit down and tell you what's going on."

Mick comes into the dining room and sits down next to me. He stretches his legs out and crosses his arms.

Yeesh, Mr. Intimidation.

"So, Samson is your partner?" I ask.

Mick nods his head yes, his mouth in a tight line.

Cynthia comes in with a beer and hands it to Mick. Constance is right behind her, and they sit down across from us and clasp their hands on the table.

"Okay. I know you're going to find this hard to believe, but it's the truth and Catherine and Cynthia will vouch for me." I sigh and decide to just blurt it out. "I have premonitions. I've had them since I was seven. All of a sudden, I'll see things in my brain, like watching scenes from a movie, only these scenes are about people and places I know, and they're about to take place in the future."

Mick doesn't say a thing but is watching me closely.

"This whole thing started when I had a premonition about Catherine a few days ago," I continue. "I saw her going into her boss's office, and then the scene changed and I saw Sampson looking at a picture of her. I could feel the danger so naturally when Catherine told me there was a contract out on her, I thought Samson was Dusty. That's why I threw the carafe of coffee at him."

"It's true," Catherine nods her head. "Constance has had visions and premonitions almost all her life."

"One of my problems is that my visions aren't always crystal clear. The scenes can change, and like in this instance, I couldn't tell if Samson was close to Catherine or across the street. I only saw him smiling and looking menacing," I explain. "I had another vision this morning. We knew you were coming into town before you got here because I saw you getting off a Harley-Davidson motorcycle in front of Pancho & Lefty's."

Mick raises his eyebrows in surprise.

"I saw your face and later I recognized you at the Sagebrush waiting for your room

77

key," I continue. "At first I thought you were Dusty, but Catherine said you didn't fit the description Jack gave her yesterday. So we thought you were another man sent by the mob to whack Catherine. That's why Catherine and I broke into your room—we were trying to find out who you are. We couldn't find anything so we followed you to the marina and onto the boat. I thought you were pulling out a gun to whack Catherine, so that's why I knocked you overboard."

Mick narrows his eyes at me. "Good thing you didn't find my gun hidden in the room. If you had, you would've shot yourself in the foot." He rolls his eyes toward Catherine. "Or Catherine's."

I sigh deeply and ignore his comment. "When we got back to the house, Catherine found the faxes from her boss with pictures of you and Dusty. That's when we discovered you're Catherine's new bodyguard, and that's the end of my story."

There's dead silence and we're all watching Mick. He purses his lips and looks at each of us.

"You," he says, pointing to Catherine. "Black pantsuit, black sun hat, and silver high heels, right?"

Catherine shakes her head yes.

"And you." This time he points to Cynthia. "Blue hair, turban, flowery pants, and sandals."

Cynthia nods her head.

Mick looks at me. "And you had on the pink wig, sexy tight pants, and white sunglasses."

Yikes! Sexy pants?

Mick gets up and hooks his thumbs in his front pockets. He walks around the table and then turns to stare at us.

"What in the hell were you ladies doing dressed up like that? It's obvious those aren't your normal clothes."

"Constance had her vision of you at a psychic's house this morning in Granby," Cynthia tells him. "We went to see if she could foresee Catherine's future. We ran into some...er...problems, and we're going back on Monday. She gave us some disguises to wear so Dusty wouldn't recognize us if we ran into him in Grand Lake, and so we could try to find out who you were."

Mick shakes his head. "Samson warned me about you ladies."

He turns and looks at me and raises one eyebrow. "I'm a little skeptical about your premonition story. I don't believe in all that paranormal and voodoo crap, but I like to keep an open mind. However, I am curious about one thing. What in the hell is butt DNA?"

NINETEEN

Dusty smokes several cigarettes in his room before he grabs the map and car keys and heads out the door. Time to scope out the area and find the house.

He turns the Cadillac toward town and drives down Grand Avenue. A mile or so past the historic main street, the road dead-ends into the parking lot going to the East Inlet Trail, and he pulls in and parks. He starts hiking down West Portal Road, which turns into the narrow trail that meanders around the lake and behind the house he's looking for.

The day is warm and sunny, and Dusty notices all the tourists and hikers in shorts, T-shirts, boots, and tennis shoes. His own leather shoes aren't easy to walk in, and as he climbs the trail, he slips and slides over the rocks and pebbles. It's getting hot and he stops to roll up the sleeves of his dress shirt.

Thirty minutes later he's tired and thirsty. He's covered in sweat and he can feel it trickle down his neck and back. His shirt is sopping wet and he pulls it out of his pants. He meets several hikers coming from the other direction, and he notes their water bottles and walking sticks with envy.

As the afternoon wears on, Dusty is breathing hard and getting exhausted. The sun is relentlessly beating down on him. He stops by a huge rock and pulls out his map.

"Need some help, fella?" a hiker coming up behind him asks.

"Yeah." Dusty barely has enough oxygen to talk. "I'm hikin' to this Rainbow Bridge. Do ya know how far it is from here?"

The hiker looks down at the map and points to their location. "We're right here. Oh, I see you have a mark on the map. Is that where you're going?"

"Yeah, I got some friends who own the house right there. I thought about stoppin' to see them on my way to the bridge."

"Hmmm, you're still several miles away. This trail runs into Jerico Road, and I think that's the house before you get to the road. Maybe it'd be a good idea if you did stop. You don't look like you hike much."

"Yeah, that's what I plan on doin'."

"Like I said, before you reach Jerico Road, you'll need to cut to the right down toward the lake. I don't think you'll have any problem finding the house. Here, take this bottle of water. I've got another in my backpack. Good luck."

Dusty grabs the water and mumbles thanks as the hiker moves on at a brisk pace. He drinks the water greedily and pours what's left over his head. Who'd of thought hiking could be so much work?

The sun is sinking in the western sky when he finally reaches Jerico Road. His clothes are limp with sweat, and he has several rips and tears in his new shirt and pants. He stops for a quick break before he turns right off the trail and toward the lake. Soon he's deep in the woods, but he keeps the shoreline in view.

Twigs and dead branches grab at his clothes and he bats at them impatiently. Finally, he sees a house in the distance.

He notices a huge pine tree in front of him. If he climbs up to one of the higher branches, he'll be able to look down on the house. He decides to give it a try and grabs the lowest branch and pulls himself up. Pinesap clings to him and the bark scratches his hands, but he keeps going. It takes him some time, but finally he's high enough to see the house, and he leans back against the trunk to catch his breath.

Dusty is rewarded for his efforts when he looks down and sees three women moving about on a patio some distance to his left. He pulls out a small pair of binoculars from his pocket and zooms in on the trio. He recognizes Catherine James and her two friends and can hear them talking, but they're too far away to catch their conversation. A few minutes later the women go in the house.

Dusty doesn't know this, but his hot, sweaty body is attracting all the ticks in the pine tree. Countless little bugs are climbing up his legs, looking for the dark, moist crevices they love. They're so tiny he doesn't feel them, but soon they're all over his body, digging their heads into his damp flesh, feeding on his blood. And they're coming in droves.

But he does notice the wasps flying around his head. He swats at a few, but instead of chasing them away, all he does is piss them off and they attack and sting. He yelps and struggles to a lower branch to try to get away. He looks around and sees their nest not too far from him.

The stings are swelling, and Dusty is hot, tired, and now angry. He keeps swatting and the wasps keep buzzing, and he gets stung again and again. The wasps continue their relentless attack, and out of desperation he takes out his pistol and aims for the nest. He shoots it, and in seconds he's covered with a furious swarm of wasps. He screams and falls out of the tree.

A large rock breaks his fall, and he hears the crack and feels the searing pain when his left arm breaks. He lays stunned for a moment, but then realizes that the gunshot is going to draw unwanted attention, so he pulls himself up and crawls back to the trail as quickly as possible.

He's half-delirious, holding his left arm, and swollen from wasp stings when he stumbles out of the woods onto the narrow trail in front of four shocked teenage boys.

TWENTY

Mick, Catherine, Cynthia, and I are eating dinner in the dining room, trying to convince Mick I'm not a nutcase, when we hear a gunshot. The three of us scream and fall to the floor as Mick bolts out the front door. We crawl into the den on our hands and knees and huddle behind the couch. Every few seconds we peek out the large window to stare at the woods behind the house.

"I think the shot came from back there," I tell my friends.

"That's what I think too," says Cynthia.

It's twilight and the sunlight is fading fast.

"Should we turn on the yard lights for Mick?" Catherine asks.

"Maybe," I say.

We're quiet and listening for any unusual noises, like a dyslexic mobster running through the woods. Or even worse, running across the porch into the house.

"Where's the switch for the yard lights?" Cynthia asks.

"Right there by the back door," I tell her.

"That one right there?" she asks, pointing with her head.

"Yep."

"The one right by that big window?"

"Yep."

"The one with three switches on it?"

"Yep."

"The one that someone would have to stand up to reach?"

"Yep."

"Exposing themselves to getting shot?"

"Yep."

I sigh. It's getting dark, and I know we need to turn on the yard lights. "I'll do it."

I belly crawl across the room to the back door, quickly stand up, and switch on the lights, drop down to the floor, and belly crawl back to my friends.

We're watching the back woods so intently, we don't hear Mick come through the front door behind us. We're softly whispering to one another.

"Do you think Mick's okay?" I ask.

"I don't know," Catherine says. "He's been gone a long time."

"I hope he doesn't get lost in the dark," Cynthia whispers.

"I don't think he's the kind of man who gets lost anywhere," I retort.

"Ladies, I'm not lost. I'm right here," Mick whispers loudly behind us.

We grab one another and scream bloody murder.

"That's payback for my swim this afternoon," he tells us when we stop screaming.

"That's mean!" Cynthia pouts. "You're supposed to be protecting us, not giving us heart attacks."

"I couldn't resist," Mick says with a big smile. "But let me make it up to you. I'll be the

85

bartender if you three ladies want to belly up to the bar, and I'll give you my report."

We move over and collapse on the barstools.

"Did you find anything in the woods?" Catherine asks him.

"No. It was hard to tell what direction the shot came from. I didn't see anyone, but I'm going to look around more tomorrow when it gets daylight. It could've been kids with a cherry bomb or big firecracker. It's getting close to July Fourth and the time for a lot of fireworks."

I get up and close the blinds in the den, turn off the yard lights, and lock the doors.

"Is your boat secured for the night?" I ask Mick.

"Yep, I did that before I came in."

"What about your motorcycle? Do you have it locked up somewhere in town?"

"I left it at the police station parking lot after I convinced them I wasn't some gun-wielding maniac."

I grimace and sit back down at the bar.

"Okay, what would you like to drink?" he asks.

We all three say at the same time, "Lemon Drop Martini."

"Do you know how to make them?" Cynthia asks.

"Sure do. I bartend in my spare time—help a friend out at a local pub."

We watch as he takes fresh lemons from a bowl on the counter and squeezes the juice out of them. He takes three martini glasses out of the bar cabinet and dips the rims in sugar. Then he pours liquor in a shaker with the juice and ice, stirs, and expertly pours the mixture in our glasses and sets them in front of us.

"If this is good, I may forgive you for scaring the bejesus out of me," I tell him. I take a sip and raise an eyebrow. "Not bad."

He scowls. "Not bad? They're damn good and you know it."

Now that makes me grin.

He pours a whiskey and sits down at the bar with us. Soon we're chatting and laughing and drinking martinis until late in the night.

TWENTY-ONE

When I open my eyes the next morning, the sun is high in the sky. My tongue feels like cotton stuck to the roof of my mouth, and my head is pounding.

I slowly pull myself out of the bed and stand up. There's a glass of ice water on my nightstand with two aspirin, and I wonder for a moment if there's such a thing as a hangover fairy before I grab the pills and swallow them with the cold water. Then I stumble out of my bedroom and down the stairs.

I follow the smell of fresh coffee to the kitchen, and when I come through the door, someone hands me a cup. I grunt and with eyes half closed continue to the counter and pour some cream in my coffee before I finally sit down at the breakfast table and take a sip. It's heavenly. I sit for a few minutes without making a sound, and when I finally lift my eyes, I see Mick leaning against a counter smiling at me.

"What?" I ask him.

He shakes his head and pours another cup of coffee.

Cynthia stumbles into the kitchen and he hands her the coffee. She takes it without a word and heads for the chair next to mine. Minutes later he repeats the process for Catherine, and soon we're all sitting in the breakfast nook. Mick brings the coffeepot over, puts it in the middle of the table, and sits down with us.

"Are you the hangover fairy?" I ask him. "The one who put aspirin and ice water by my bed?"

"That would be me," he answers. "I put them in all your rooms this morning. Somehow I knew you'd need them."

"So, you're a private investigator, bodyguard, bartender, and hangover fairy." Catherine counts them off on her fingers. "Pretty impressive."

"I'm not too fond of the term 'fairy,'" he tells us.

The oven dings and Mick gets up. He grabs a hot pad and pulls out a pan.

"Breakfast frittata," he says as he gets plates from the cabinet. He pulls another pan out of the oven. "Biscuits."

He dishes everything up and puts a plate in front of each of us, then fills one for himself and sits back down. We all dig in.

"We can add gourmet chef to that list," Cynthia tells him with her mouth half full. "This is good."

We eat in congenial silence for a few minutes before Mick breaks the serenity.

"So, what's on the agenda for today, ladies? Wreaking havoc on some poor, unsuspecting soul in the village, or running amok and causing chaos with the lake habitat?"

"Ha, ha," I say. "Maybe we'll take it easy today, cruise around the lake in the boat or do some kayaking."

"Did you check the woods this morning?" Catherine asks.

"Sure did," Mick answers. He refills his coffee cup and leans back in his chair. "I found some broken branches and bits of clothing stuck to bushes not far from the main trail back there." He frowns. "I didn't find any shoe tracks, but it's been real dry up here, and no sign of firecrackers either. If it was a gunshot we heard last evening, I don't think it was pointed toward the house. I couldn't find any bullet holes or evidence of anything being shot at around here, but that doesn't mean it didn't happen."

"Hmmm. Since we haven't seen or heard anything from Dusty, I'm hoping he's given up," Cynthia says. She stands and stretches, then grabs the empty dishes from the table and goes to the sink. "I'll load the dishwasher and clean the kitchen since you cooked, Mick. Thanks for taking care of breakfast."

"My pleasure." He scoots his chair back and heads for the front door. "I think I'll look around some more. Don't anyone leave the house until I get back." He stops with his hand on the doorknob and turns to glare at us. "And I mean that. No one leave this house. Not to take out trash, sit on the patio, feed the ducks, or go to your little water garage. Stay inside."

He pulls a card from his pocket—of course it's wavy and has watermarks on it from his dunk in the lake the day before—and hands it to me.

"My cell phone number is on there. Call me if anything happens, or if you have one of those…little inspirations of yours."

"Premonitions," I tell him. "They're premonitions."

"Yeah, whatever." He grins and is gone.

"That man is beginning to be a pain in my ass," I tell my friends.

TWENTY-TWO

After cleaning the kitchen, we go upstairs to shower and dress. I put on some yoga crops and a tank top, and wrap a jacket around my waist before shoving my feet into my favorite tennis shoes. I step out to my balcony to let my hair finish drying and find Catherine sitting in one of the lounge chairs.

Birds are singing, bees are buzzing, and flowers are blooming in the beautiful woods below us.

"It sure is peaceful up here," Catherine sighs.

I sit beside her and run fingers through my hair. "Sure is."

A minute later Cynthia joins us.

"Would you two like to take a boat ride around the lakes today?" I ask them.

"Sure," answers Cynthia. "I'd like that. And maybe later we could do some kayaking."

"Oh yeah, let's do both," says Catherine.

We sit for a few minutes enjoying the quiet when Cynthia grunts. "Umm, is sitting on the balcony considered in or out of the house?" she asks.

I groan. "Oh, crap. Mick is going to have a conniption if he sees us out here. Let's go in before he finds us."

We rush back in and meet in the den. Mick is drinking coffee at the bar.

"We're going for a boat ride. Wanna join us?" I ask as I grab the key to the Moomba off the rack by the door, along with my favorite baseball cap.

"Sure!" He jumps up and follows us out the door.

"Is all secure here at Camp Bootie?" I ask him.

"Yep, all's well."

"I'll bring the boat around," I tell them as I head for the garage.

"I'll help you," Mick offers.

I turn to tell him I don't need his help when I see Catherine and Cynthia behind him making goo-goo eyes and signaling me to let him go.

I cross my eyes and stick my tongue out at them, which is real grown-up, I know.

I put in the code to the garage door and when it opens, I slip inside, untie the Moomba, and climb in. Mick gets in and I back the boat out and pull it up to the pier. When Cynthia and Catherine are settled in the back, I pull the throttle down, and we take off across the smooth lake.

It's a gorgeous day and the spray on my face is exhilarating and delightful.

"Have you ever been to Grand Lake?" I ask Mick. I have to yell to be heard over the motor.

"Several times on my bike, but I've never been in a boat on the lake before," he yells back.

I slow the boat down and head for the shoreline so I can give everyone a tour of Grand Lake and be heard without hollering.

I show them where the East Inland Trailhead and Adam Falls are, then we head toward the village, and I point out several of the older homes on the lake. We pass the marina and Point Park, going through the passage under Rainbow Bridge and following the canal around to Shadow Mountain Lake.

We honk and wave at other boats, kayakers, and fishermen along the shore. When we get to the open waters, I speed up and we head for one of the many islands on Shadow Mountain Lake while avoiding the waterskiers.

I point to several osprey nests and then pull up to an island so we can tie up and look around.

We jump out, and Cynthia and Catherine take off to try and capture the osprey with their cameras.

"You can go with them if you want," I tell Mick. "I'll stay here with the boat."

"Nah, I'm not a bird watcher, and I think Catherine will be safe."

I sit on a fallen pine tree in the shade and Mick joins me.

"Nice boat," he observes while we wait for the photographers to return. "You ski?"

"Some. I bought the boat for my kids, grandkids, and nieces and nephews. They ski, but mostly now I ride on the big tube with the smaller kids."

"Sounds like fun."

"It is, but it takes a lot of energy. I'm not as young as I used to be."

"You look like you do okay."

I grunt. "This lake isn't as cold as Grand Lake, which is why you see all the waterskiers over here. Grand Lake is the deepest natural lake in Colorado and freezing. But Shadow Mountain is pretty darn cold too, which is why we usually wear wet suits when we ski and tube."

"I sure could've used one yesterday."

I cringe. "I'm so sorry about knocking you out of the boat yesterday, Mick. I'm never gonna live that down, am I?"

He shrugs and smiles. "Maybe you can make it up to me sometime."

I don't know what to say to that, so I shut up.

"So, you're divorced, right?" he asks.

"Yeah, for about ten years."

"Anyone special in your life?"

I think a minute. "My kids, grandkids, Catherine, Cynthia, my neighbors, and a few other friends. What about you?"

"Been divorced for over fifteen years, no kids, and not dating anyone right now. My line of work consumes most of my time, so I don't have much of a social life."

"That's too bad," I tell him and mean it. I can't imagine life without the chaos that my kids and grandkids bring to it. Not to mention my two BFFs. "Have you always been a private investigator?"

"No, I was a detective with the Denver Police in my previous life. I retired several years ago and started the PI business with my old partner, Samson."

"Oh yes. Dear ol' Sampson. How's he doing?"

"I talked to him this morning. He's out of the hospital and back to work. I told him what happened yesterday—that gave him a good laugh."

"Yeah, it was a real riot."

Mick chuckles. "Oh, don't be so hard on yourself. You thought you were protecting your friend. But you sure pack a punch, lady."

It's my turn to smile. "I play a lot of water volleyball in the summer—builds up my upper arm strength."

Catherine and Cynthia come back all excited about their pictures of the osprey and chipmunks. We board the Moomba and head back to Grand Lake.

"This has been the quietest day we've had all week," Cynthia observes when we're back at the house.

"I sure hope it stays that way," Catherine retorts.

"Don't jinx it, the day's not over," I tell them.

After a late lunch of sandwiches and iced tea on the patio, I head for the small garage on the side of the house.

"It's a nice evening for kayaking," I tell the group. "Or we can take a ride on the mountain bikes if you'd rather stay on land."

"I think I'd rather kayak," Catherine says. "I'm not too interested in riding a bike back in those woods."

"I'll kayak too, if you have enough," Cynthia offers.

"We have four, so everyone can kayak if they want."

"I better go too," Mick grumbles. "Let's try to stay together, if that's possible."

We haul the kayaks out and lay them on the shore by the pier.

"Cynthia, Catherine, and I have all kayaked before," I say. "Have you, Mick?"

"I think I can manage," he mumbles as he puts a life jacket on.

"Oh, wait," Catherine calls. "I forgot the old bagels we're going to feed to the ducks."

She runs into the house and comes back with several plastic bags, handing one to each of us. We push off in the kayaks and soon we're paddling along the shore.

The late-afternoon sun is fading as we quietly glide across the peaceful lake. No one says anything, and the tranquility is broken only by the calls of the osprey and other birds as we paddle along enjoying nature at its best. Occasionally someone points at a fish jumping out of the water, or some mountain flowers on the banks.

We come around a bend and meet up with a group of ducks. Or is it a herd of ducks? Anyway, it's a lot of ducks, so we start throwing out pieces of the stale bagels. And before my eyes, that group of ducks grows. I don't know where they're all coming from, but suddenly there are ducks everywhere. Big ducks, little ducks, mama ducks, baby ducks, and they're all wrestling for the bagels. I didn't know ducks could be so aggressive.

"Yikes! Throw them all the bagels and let's get out of here," I yell.

I fling my bagels in the air, and I'm horrified to see them land on Mick. Immediately all the ducks zero in on him. Several big drakes are squawking and flapping in his face, and the next thing I see is Mick flipping over and falling in the lake.

"Man overboard," I shout.

Cynthia and Catherine start throwing their bagels in the opposite direction, and seconds later the mob of ducks is scurrying away from us.

Catherine and I paddle toward Mick, who's hanging onto his upside-down kayak, and we're able to turn the kayak right side up. We manage to push the kayak toward shore, and Mick swims after us.

"I'm so sorry, Mick," I moan. "I didn't see you behind me when I threw my bagels."

"You're right about one thing," he growls. "This lake is damn cold."

TWENTY-THREE

We paddle back to the house and drag the kayaks up by the garage. It's dusk and the automatic lights come on.

Catherine, Cynthia, and I march through the front door like good little soldiers, with Mick behind us not saying a word. The silence is deafening.

He walks to the bar, grabs a glass and the whiskey decanter, and turns to face us.

"I'm going up to take a hot shower. No one leave the house."

When he's out of sight, we breathe a sigh of relief.

"Oh crap, he's mad," Cynthia comments. "And who can blame him? That's twice he's been dunked in the lake."

"It's not like we plan for these things to happen. We just seem to attract trouble these days." Catherine sighs, then pokes me. "He's kinda cute when he gives you 'the look.' You know, that smirky, half-grin kinda look."

I turn and give Catherine "the look."

"Yeah, that's the one, girlfriend. You got it."

"You mean the one where he can't decide if he wants to spank us or strangle us?" I stop and gasp. "I can't believe I said spank! I'm reading *Fifty Shades of Grey*, and now it's creeping into my vocabulary."

"You're reading that too?" Cynthia asks me. "I started it last night."

"Oh God, I can't believe this. I'm reading *Fifty Shades* too," Catherine exclaims.

We look at each other and grin.

"Well, great minds, and all that," Cynthia observes. "Or else we spend way too much time together and we're starting to think alike."

"When have we ever spent too much time together?" I ask with a smile. "And I can't believe we're all reading erotica, or that I'm sixty and I've never heard of half of this stuff."

"If nothing else, we're a well-read group," Catherine comments. "Speaking of books, I think this is a good time for me to go up to my room and read another chapter, but first I want to call my kids." She heads for her room.

"Yeah, I think I'll go upstairs and try to Skype Dave on my laptop," Cynthia tells me.

I decide to touch base with my kids and wander out to the back porch with my cell phone. I catch up with my son and daughter and grandkids, carefully omitting the real reason I'm in Grand Lake with Catherine and Cynthia so as not to worry them, and then walk back into the den.

Mick is sitting on the couch and has exchanged his whiskey for a cup of coffee. "Feeling better?" I ask him.

"Lots." He takes a sip and stares at me over his cup. "So much for not leaving the house."

I roll my eyes, which I know is so *Fifty Shades*.

"Ya know, Mick, we normally don't cause this much trouble—I mean, I don't know what's going on—maybe there's a disturbance in the cosmos, or the planets are all in alignment, or out of alignment or something. Actually, we live calm, happy, uneventful lives, and Catherine *never* has contracts out on her, trust me."

He grunts. "You three women can cause mayhem just by walking in a room. I've never seen anything like it. I'd put someone else on this case, but I'm afraid of what you might do to him."

I grimace. "Well, we'll give you a break and retire to our rooms for the night. I brought my Kindle and plan on reading this evening. You can have the den and big-screen television to yourself. How does that sound?"

I'm surprised when Mick smiles and tells me, "Boring." He shakes his head. "At least there's never a dull moment with you three. Except for putting my partner in the hospital and my dunks in the lake, you ladies are a lot of fun. I never know what to expect, and you're a breath of fresh air."

I stare at him, my mouth wide open. "Really?"

"Yep, really. And I wouldn't put anyone else on this case because I'd hate to miss out on what happens next. As long as I can keep you all safe, especially Catherine, and I can only do that if you'll listen to me. Please, don't go out on the porch by yourself again, okay?"

I sigh. "Sorry, I forgot. I was trying to get better cell reception so I could call my kids.

Next time I'll use the landline in the office if I can't get my cell phone to work."

Catherine and Cynthia come into the den. "We're exhausted and thinking of calling it a day," they tell us.

"Really?" I ask them, raising my eyebrows. I know what they're up to, the little connivers.

"I thought you might like a fast game of Scrabble or Monopoly, although I think Mick here would prefer a game of poker," I suggest with a grin.

Cynthia raises her eyebrows with interest. "Five card stud or Texas hold'em?" she asks.

"Texas hold'em," Mick tells her.

Cynthia goes behind the bar, grabs a deck of cards, and then sits down at the game table by the fireplace. We all join her as she hands the cards to Mick.

"Deal," she tells him.

Ha! I knew I had the little card shark at poker.

TWENTY-FOUR

The next morning we wake up to coffee and pancakes, compliments of Mick. What a guy.

"Well, we've done 'wreaking havoc on unsuspecting villagers' and 'causing chaos with the wildlife' to death. What does everyone want to do today?" I ask when we finish cleaning our plates.

"What's left to do?" Catherine asks with a chuckle.

"We could try and find Dusty and beat the crap out of him," Cynthia tells us. "We haven't done that yet."

Mick leans back in his chair with a thoughtful expression. "Now that would be interesting. I can only imagine what you three are capable of doing to him without even trying."

"Huh," I grunt. "It's Saturday and there's a big craft show in town this weekend. We haven't spent much time shopping or soaking up Grand Lake's ambiance, so maybe we could spend today doing that."

"Hmm." Now it's Mick's turn to grunt. "It's going to be crowded in town. That may be a problem with trying to protect Catherine from Dusty."

"What if we wear disguises again? Not the ones we wore before," Cynthia says emphatically. "Something simpler. Like, why don't we dress up in sun hats or baseball caps with sunglasses, or I don't know, crazy T-shirts or something?"

"That might work," Mick says thoughtfully.

"I don't know about crazy T-shirts, but there's a ton of Boulder Bolder shirts up here," I tell them. "Sam runs it every year. We could wear those with shorts, pull our hair back in ponytails, and put on ball caps."

"Sure, and then we can put on shades," Catherine chimes in. "Maybe that will hide our faces enough so Dusty won't recognize me or any of us."

An hour later we're dressed and ready to leave, and I have the Moomba waiting.

"Want to drive?" I ask Mick when we're all in.

"Oh yes," he tells me, and we trade places.

We circle around the lake a few times and Mick is grinning from ear to ear. Finally he heads for the marina. It's crowded but we find a slot and ease the Moomba in, tie her up, and jump out.

We spend the next two hours cruising up and down Grand Avenue, going in and out of all the little gift shops. Then we meander around the town park area where the craft tents are set up.

For lunch we stop at Grumpy's, the best hamburger joint in the village, and then continue our shopping marathon.

"I can't believe you ladies haven't bought anything yet," Mick grumbles.

"We don't want to carry packages around all day, so we're waiting until we leave to get what we want," Catherine tells him.

Mick raises his eyebrows and looks at his watch. "It's five o'clock, how much longer are you going to shop?"

"I guess we could buy a few things now," Cynthia says.

"Why don't we do that and then we can go to the Lariat Saloon for a beer and bite to eat before we leave," I suggest.

An hour later we're coming out of the Red Sled Boutique when we see the Grand Lake Mini Cooper barreling down the street.

"Uh-oh," I tell everyone. "That's not a good sign."

Sure enough. When the Cooper gets right up to us, we hear, *"Moose alert. Moose alert! Moose on the loose! Everyone take cover!"* coming out of the speakers on top of the little car.

And right behind the Cooper is a big bull moose trotting down the middle of Grand Avenue. People are screaming and running for their lives on both sides of the street.

"Quick!" I yell. "We're only a block or two from the Lariat. Let's take cover there."

The moose must've heard me, and I dunno, maybe he wants an ice-cold beer too, because he stops and looks our way. Then he lowers his head with a loud snort, and charges toward us.

"Oh, shit—run!" I shriek.

Cynthia, Catherine, and Mick take off running on their long legs, and I'm right behind them on my short, squatty ones.

Minutes later we're sprinting through the door to the Lariat with a dozen other people. And in seconds we see the bull moose wander past us on his way down the middle of the street, looking for some unsuspecting tourists to terrorize.

"Amazing," Cynthia and Catherine say together.

"He's beautiful, and so big," Cynthia continues, a little breathless.

"Oh yeah, he's big, and beautiful from a distance," I gasp. I sink down in a stool by the bar and hold my chest.

"Let's get a beer and a brat or something while we're waiting for the all clear," Mick suggests after the moose is out of sight. "And we'll let Constance catch her breath."

I narrow my eyes at Mick, and I shift between delirious laughter and uncontrollable cackling.

"Oh sure, make fun of me, but let me tell you that those animals are unpredictable, and can attack at the least provocation, as you can tell from what just happened. We're lucky to be alive." It's obvious to me Mick didn't have an inkling of the danger we were in.

In a half daze, I turn in my stool and recognize Patty, one of the main weekend bartenders, on duty.

"Hey!" Patty greets me. "I haven't seen you in awhile. How ya been doing?"

"I'm doing great now, Patty. I'm up here with some friends for a few days. How's business?" I'm still breathing hard.

"Can't complain." She slides a beer to the guy sitting next to me. "So, what can I get for you all?"

"Beers, and real quick," I tell her.

She grins and pours us all a draft. We order nachos and burritos, and then Catherine and Cynthia drift off to look around the saloon. The walls are covered with posters, bumper stickers, and license plates, and the place is buzzing with conversation and energy.

Mick sits next to me when Catherine vacates her seat.

"I take it you've been here before, right?" I ask him, now that my heart rate is back to normal.

"Many times. I bike with a group, and every summer we make at least one trip up here, stop for lunch, and then head back to Denver."

"Have you ever been here at night?"

"No, can't say that I have."

"Interesting place, especially on a Saturday night. It really rocks."

Patty smiles at me and nods in agreement.

"Who's playing tonight?" I ask Patty.

"Jim and Al. You remember them?"

"Oh, most definitely. When do they start?"

"Probably around seven or eight. You staying?"

"I'm not sure. It depends on what everyone wants to do."

Mick looks around the saloon. "Do they dance here?" he asks.

"Yes, Jim and Al set up in front of that pool table, and we scoot the tables and chairs over a bit to make room," Patty tells him.

"Do you dance?" I ask Mick.

"I've been known to dance a little," he says with a smile.

"Jim and Al take requests if you want to hear anything special. They're good. Jim plays a synthesizer thingy, and Al plays the guitar and banjo."

"Maybe we need to stick around then. You could make it up to me with a dance." His smile widens.

"Make what up?" I ask with a dare in my eyes. Didn't he run past me not fifteen minutes ago, leaving me at the mercy of Bullwinkle the Moose?

Mick raises his eyebrows and gives me "the look."

Catherine and Cynthia come back to the bar, and I'm relieved because I'm not quite sure how to interpret Mick's "look." Is it the "I want to spank you" look, or the "I want to strangle you" look?

Patty puts our plates on the bar, along with our drafts of Coors Light. It doesn't take us long to scarf down our food, and when we finish, we sit and sip our beer and watch the crowd come in. The doors open, and I hear the shouts as patrons greet Jim. A few minutes later

Al comes through the door and there's more shouts.

Jim and Al are known not only for their great music, but also for their pranks. And sure enough, I know they're setting someone up for one of their favorites, and I'm sure it's me. But I know what's coming.

Jim comes over, puts his arms around me, and gives me a big bear hug and smooch on the cheek. "Hey, Constance! Ready for some fun?" he asks.

"Sure," I tell him.

Then Mick makes a big mistake. He gets up and stands right behind me.

"Hey, Patty! Give me a hit," Jim hollers.

Patty grins and pulls the water tap out from behind the bar. That's when Jim and I duck at the same time, and Patty squirts Mick right in the face.

TWENTY-FIVE

Mick is a good sport about the prank. Patty gives him a bar towel to dry off with because he's drenched.

I can't help myself. I'm laughing like a loon. Catherine and Cynthia are laughing hysterically too, along with everyone in the bar. I don't know what it is about Mick and water, but he's a magnet for H20.

When I pull myself together, I feel bad, but only for a second. Actually, I don't feel bad at all because I'm still a little peeved at Mick. I knew the water prank was meant for me, and I'm delighted I turned the tables on Jim. If Mick had stayed in his chair, he would've been okay and some poor schmuck behind me would've gotten it. But God! It's so funny that Mick was the schmuck!

"Oh, Mick. Are you okay?" I ask, trying to catch my breath and stop laughing.

"You knew that was coming, didn't you?"

"Yes, I've seen Jim and Al work the bar prank before. But why did you get up and move? You'd been okay if you'd stayed seated."

Mick laughs and looks sheepish.

"I think it's because of my natural instincts to protect my clients. When Jim came up and started manhandling you, I got nervous."

I look at him, surprised. "Manhandling?"

110

"Well, yeah. That's what it looked like to me."

I don't know what to say, so I shut up. Again.

Mick seems relieved when Patty interrupts and places a draft of Coors Light on the bar.

"This one is on the house," she tells Mick.

"Thanks." He smiles at her. "Good shot."

"I do my best." She grins and moves on down the bar.

"Sorry, pal." Jim puts his hand on Mick's shoulder. "I was aiming to get ol' Constance here, but she's too smart for me. Bad timing on your part. But hey, let me know if you have any special requests, okay?"

"Sure," Mick tells him. "I'll do that."

"Are you guys up for a game of pool?" Cynthia asks.

"I am," Catherine tells her.

"Me too. What about you, Mick?" I ask.

Mick looks at us suspiciously. "Are you ladies pool sharks?" he asks.

We laugh.

"Noooo," Catherine answers. "Cynthia and Dave have a big game room with a billiards table, and we play there some. What makes you think we're pool sharks?"

"Oh, I don't know. Maybe because you're all so damn good at poker. You beat the socks off me last night."

"Well, good thing we weren't playing strip poker, huh? But we're only marginally good at pool," Cynthia purrs.

"Yeah, right. Nah, I'll pass. Besides, the music is going to start any minute."

And right on cue, Jim and Al started playing, "Old Time Rock N' Roll."

"Never mind. Let's dance," Catherine whoops.

We all jump up and start dancing.

TWENTY-SIX

Dusty is released from the Granby Hospital on Saturday night. He hires a cab to take him to the trailhead parking lot, where his car is parked. He picks it up, and on his way to the Grand Lake Lodge, he passes the Lariat Saloon and hears all the whooping and hollering through the open windows.

It's a good thing he told the lodge that he wanted the room for several days and left the checkout open, or they would have rented it out. As it is, they aren't too happy with him.

"We know you were smoking in your room, Mr. Galucci," the hotel manager tells him sternly when he gets there. "As you know, we have a strict no-smoking rule in this lodge. Since it's your first visit, we'll let it pass this time, but we must insist that you abide by our regulations. Otherwise, we'll have no choice but to evict you from our premises."

If Dusty wasn't so desperate to get to his room and fall into bed, he would've told the SOB to go to hell, shot him in the foot, and left. But all he can do is passively nod in agreement. He knows he looks pathetic in his sweat-stained and torn clothes, but at least the swelling from the wasp stings has gone down. Except for a few black and blue marks left by the stingers, he looks halfway normal, even with his left arm in a cast.

After agreeing to extend his reservations for an additional week, and promising to pay for the room to be professionally cleaned and an expensive air filter installed, he finally gets to his room. He takes off his clothes and crawls into bed exhausted.

The whole hospital experience was another thing entirely, and Dusty can't stop reliving it—every humiliating and embarrassing second he spent there. Not only did they have to give him a shitload of Benadryl to reduce the swelling from the wasp stings, but they also had to set his broken arm, which hurt like hell.

But the worst was the hours it took for the nursing staff to remove all the ticks embedded in his body. Most of the ticks were in his butt crack and around his balls and dick, and he watched the nurses through his swollen eyes as they worked to remove the little monsters. Although they were fairly quiet while they labored, he could see the looks that passed from one to another, and hear the tsking through their pursed lips.

The only thing that helped him get through the whole ordeal was thinking about how much pleasure he would have when he finally put a bullet through the head of that James broad.

And his pleasure would be tripled because he was going to save two bullets for her friends and watch them die together.

TWENTY-SEVEN

It's Sunday morning and for some reason I'm tired. Oh yeah, it's because we danced the night away at the Lariat Saloon. And because I'm sixty years old and not used to dancing the night away.

I crawl out of bed and down the stairs to the kitchen for a cup of coffee. Mick has us all spoiled, and it's no surprise when he puts a cup in my hand as I walk through the door.

"Morning, Mick," I greet him sleepily. I sniff the air and recognize the scent of cinnamon rolls in our future. Life is sweet.

Cynthia and Catherine are already sitting at the table drinking coffee when I join them. A minute later we have cinnamon rolls in front of us. Life is not only sweet, it's good.

"So, what are you ladies going to do today?" Mick asks us.

"Rest," Catherine tells him.

"Sleep," I say.

"Read," Cynthia decides.

"That's good because I want to look around the woods some more this morning. If you're resting, sleeping, and reading, I won't have to worry about you. I may go into the village later on, so if you need any supplies make a list for me."

Mick gets up and stretches, then leaves through the kitchen door.

"He's slipping," I tell the others. "He didn't tell us to stay in the house."

"I heard that." Mick pokes his head back through the door and smirks at us. "Don't leave the house."

"Jeez, what a control freak," I groan.

We clean up the kitchen, then grab our coffee and head for the den. I curl up on the sofa with an afghan, Catherine collapses in a recliner, and Cynthia goes up to get our Kindles. Spending a quiet day reading *Fifty Shades* seems like a perfect Sunday to me.

I finish my coffee and go up to my room to shower and dress. When I come down, I settle back on the sofa with my Kindle and afghan. Minutes later, I'm sound asleep.

I stir when I hear Mick come through the back door, and sit up. Catherine and Cynthia look up from their Kindles. Mick is holding something in his hand and has a serious look on his face.

"We've had a visitor," he tells us.

I'm wide-awake now, and he has our attention.

"I found these binoculars in the woods under a big pine tree not far from the house," he goes on. "There were some broken branches under the tree, and I also found a wasp nest lying on the ground close by, with what looks like a bullet hole in it. My theory is that Dusty climbed the tree, got tangled up with the wasps, and shot their nest down. They probably swarmed him, and in his rush to get away from the little devils, he dropped his binoculars."

"Do you think that was the gunshot we heard the other night?" Catherine asks.

"Yes, very possibly. But if my theory's correct, where's Dusty? We heard the gunshot on Thursday night, nearly four days ago. If that was him, and he was snooping around, why hasn't he done something? In Denver he left a note pinned to your dead informant, and another one in your mailbox, isn't that right, Catherine?"

Catherine nods her head. "Yes. I found the second note in my mailbox the morning after they found my informant. And Jack told me on Thursday that his police connections heard Dusty was on his way up here."

"Dusty was quick to let you know you were next on the list, so why is he waiting so long to make his presence known? Where is he and what is he up to?" Mick questions. He has a worried look on his face. "The thing I'm concerned about is maybe he has someone helping him. Or maybe he's not as dumb as we think, and he's letting us get complacent, hoping we'll let our guard down, and then he'll hit when we least expect it."

"That's how Tony Soprano did it," Cynthia offers. "His victims were always caught by surprise."

"Believe it or not, that makes sense to me," Mick tells her. "I'm going in the office to call Samson. I want him to do some snooping and see what he can find out. In the meantime, it's doubly important that we keep our guard up. And no one is safe." He looks directly at Cynthia and me. "Including you two. They'd have no qualms killing you to get to Catherine."

I shiver and sink down in my afghan as I watch Mick walk toward the office.

"Where are my premonitions when I need them?" I ask softly.

"Which reminds me, I think I'll call Flavia and confirm our appointment for tomorrow," Cynthia says. "I'll use my cell upstairs." She leaves to make the call.

"It's creepy to think Dusty could've been out there in a tree watching us," Catherine murmurs. "And who knows where he is now."

I nod my head slowly. "Where are you now, Dusty Galucci?"

TWENTY-EIGHT

Mick comes back into the den at the same time Cynthia comes down the stairs.

"Flavia has us confirmed for ten o'clock tomorrow morning," she tells us.

"Who's Flavia?" Mick asks.

"Our psychic," Catherine tells him. "Do you think it'll be okay for us to go see her in Granby tomorrow?"

Mick shrugs. "Probably, but we'll have to wait and see. If anything happens, or if I think you're in danger, we'll have to leave immediately for a safe house. I have Samson securing one in Denver now as a standby."

The thought of going to a safe house shocks us into silence. At least for a minute.

"Crap," Catherine groans. "It's bad enough I'm in this mess, but now I've dragged my two best friends in with me."

"Hey, you didn't drag us, we volunteered, girlfriend," I tell her.

"Yep," Cynthia agrees. "We wouldn't want to be anywhere else. Besides, all we were told to do was hide out somewhere for a couple of weeks, remember? Everyone seemed to think this was going to blow over and Dusty would lose interest in you. Who knows? Maybe he has. That's possible, isn't it, Mick?"

"It's possible. That's one of the things I'm having Samson check out—Dusty's whereabouts. If he's back in Denver and the contract has been called off, it'll be safe for

119

everyone to go back home. But in the meantime, I'm going to boat over to the village, snoop around a little myself. If anyone needs anything, I'll be happy to pick it up while I'm there."

"Let me check to make sure we have lemons and vodka," I tell him. I get up and check the liquor cabinet and fridge. "We have plenty of both. I don't know of anything we need, do you guys?"

Catherine and Cynthia shake their heads no.

"Okay, I'll be gone for a few hours, so lock the doors, turn on the security system, and keep my cell number handy," Mick tells us.

He grabs a jacket and cap off the rack by the front door. When he turns back toward us, I raise my hand with a stop gesture.

"We know. Don't leave the house."

He grins and shuts the door.

We settle in the den with our Kindles and all is quiet.

At noon we eat some sandwiches and then go back to our reading.

I'm deeply engrossed into *Fifty Shades* when Cynthia interrupts.

"Hey, you two," she whispers loudly. "I think I see someone out in the woods."

"What! Where?" I ask.

"Over there." She points to the backyard.

All three of us creep up to the big window and scrunch down.

"There! See?" Cynthia exclaims.

120

"Omigod! It looks like a man hiding behind those trees," Catherine gasps.

"And it looks like he's dressed in some kind of camouflage," I squeal. "It's got to be Dusty! What's he doing?"

"He's sneaking up to the house, that's what he's doing. What are we going to do?" Cynthia wails.

"Quick!" I say. "One of you get Mick's card off the fridge where I stuck it under a magnet and call him. I'm going to try and find something we can defend ourselves with."

I run down to the lower level of the house to the game room. Surely there's something we can use—a baseball bat, a hockey stick, maybe golf balls or a used Wii? Crap! What did the kid use in *Home Alone*? I look though a closet filled with paraphernalia and junk and see something that might work. Two big slingshots.

I rush up the stairs and run to the kitchen, pull open the freezer, and grab several bags of frozen mini bagels. I hurry back to the den with my artillery and a plan.

"Where is he now?" I ask.

"He's going back and forth between the trees," Catherine tells me. "He's still back a ways. It's weird, but he keeps looking at the ground. Why would he do that?"

I watch him through the distant trees. "I don't know. Maybe he's looking for snakes or something."

"Mick isn't answering his cell," Cynthia interrupts us.

"Leave a message," I tell her. "Tell him to get his butt back here now."

I hear Cynthia in the background leaving a message as Catherine and I keep our eyes glued on Dusty.

"Mick!" Cynthia yells into his voice mailbox. "There's a man in the back woods. We think it's Dusty. Get your butt back here."

"Omigod! He's getting closer," Catherine gasps.

"Omigod! He's getting closer," Cynthia mimics in the phone.

"He's holding something," I cry. "Is that a rifle?"

"He's holding something, and we think it's a rifle," Cynthia repeats hysterically.

"Cynthia! For God's sake! Hang up the phone and help us," I shout. "We've gotta come up with a plan."

"Gotta go, Mick. We've gotta come up with a plan," Cynthia tells the phone, and then hangs up.

"I found these two big slingshots downstairs," I show my friends. "Cynthia, you and I will sneak out and hide behind the hot tub. When he gets close enough, we'll start shooting these frozen mini bagels at him."

"What should I do?" Catherine asks.

"When we start shooting, you need to run out the front door and find someplace to hide. Maybe in the water garage with the Moomba. You know the code. Stay in there until Mick comes."

"Wait a minute, why can't I shoot a slingshot?"

"Because we only have two."

"Well, why do I have to run into the water garage and hide?"

"Because it's *you* Dusty wants to whack."

"But what about you and Cynthia? I can't run and hide and leave you to face him with…with frozen mini bagels, for God's sake."

"Yes, you can, Catherine. And for God's sake, that's all we have! It's not like we have any spare butt plugs around this place, you know."

Catherine and Cynthia look at me with huge eyes, and then we all burst out laughing.

"I can't believe you said that," Catherine howls in laughter.

"And I can't believe we're standing here laughing when we have a hit man coming after us," Cynthia hoots.

"We're hysterical because we have a truckload of adrenaline flowing through our bloodstream right now," I tell them. "That, plus our unforgettable memories of butt plugs from *Fifty Shades*, a bag of frozen mini bagels, and some good shooting skills will get us through this, I hope. Now, Cynthia, you and I need to go hide behind the hot tub. Catherine, you keep watch inside, but get out before he comes into the house if we can't stop him."

We hug each other, and then Cynthia and I slip through the back door with our bagels and slingshots.

TWENTY-NINE

Cynthia and I huddle down behind the hot tub and watch Dusty work his way toward the house. We open the bags of bagels, which are as hard as rocks, and have our slingshots ready.

"He sure is brave coming up in the middle of the day, don'cha think?" Cynthia asks me.

"It's easier for him to see in the daylight, I suppose," I answer back. "Look! He's getting closer. We should get ready."

We watch, and when we think he's close enough, we load our slingshots.

"Are you ready, Tonto?" I ask.

"Yes, Kemo Sabe," Cynthia responds.

"Fire," I whisper loudly.

We stand, take aim, and start shooting.

It doesn't take long before Dusty starts screaming, "Hey! Stop! Stop!"

Yeah, right. Like that's going to happen.

We keep shooting as Dusty runs back and forth and tries to dodge our frozen bullets.

I get the feel of the slingshot and see a number of my bagels hit him in the head and other parts of his body. I can see that Cynthia is getting her shots in too.

"Ouch! Stop! Please," he yells.

Dusty starts running away from the house, and Cynthia and I are right behind him.

If he had a gun, he dropped it, and I'm getting braver. I'm mad now, and I could easily strangle him with the slingshot if I can catch him. Or maybe just beat the crap out of him, like Cynthia suggested the other day.

Cynthia keeps shooting, and I run after him as he zigs and zags through the woods. He looks back for a second, and when he turns around, he smacks headfirst into a low-hanging pine branch. He falls down in a heap and doesn't move.

Cynthia and I rush through the woods toward him, and I can hear Catherine screaming behind us.

"You got him!"

"Get something to tie him up with," I yell at her.

The Battle of Bootie's Hideaway is over.

We slow down when we get closer, in case he's playing possum, but he doesn't move.

We cautiously approach, and when we're next to him, we slowly reach out and turn him over on his back.

We stand back and gasp.

"Oh, shit. That's not Dusty," Cynthia cries.

She's right. And not only that, he's wearing a ranger uniform.

"Oh, shit is right," I moan. "We just brought down one of our forest rangers."

Catherine comes up with rope and looks down at the ranger.

"Oh, shit. We did it again, didn't we?"

"Oh yeah, we're three for three for taking down the wrong man," I tell her.

Our ranger groans and starts coming to. I'd like to run back to the house and pretend this never happened, but my big girl voice tells me to stay put and face the music. Plus, I want to make sure he's okay.

He sits up and puts a hand to the knot on his forehead. "What happened?" he asks. He shakes his head slowly and looks up at us.

"Sir, you ran into a tree branch and hit your head," Catherine tells him, enunciating each word carefully. "You may have a concussion."

She bends down to look at his head. Then she holds up three fingers. "How many hands am I holding up?" she asks.

The ranger looks at her confused, and then smiles slowly. "Is this a trick question? You're holding up one hand and three fingers."

Now it's Catherine's turn to look confused until she realizes what she did and does a quick recovery.

"Yes, that's right. It was a trick question and you passed. I don't think you have a concussion." She pats his leg and stands up.

"Do you think you can stand?" Cynthia asks him. "We'll help you get to your feet and take you to our house over there."

The three of us help him get up. He puts one arm around Catherine's shoulder, and we slowly move toward our back door. When we get him in the den, I rush into the kitchen to get an ice pack.

A few minutes later, he's settled in a big recliner with an ice bag on his forehead and the three of us surrounding him.

"Do you remember what happened?" I ask him.

"Yeah, it was strange. We had some reports of bears in the area, so I was out looking for scat, and the next thing I know, some kids are shooting rocks at me! That's all I remember until I came to and you ladies were leaning over me. Thanks for coming to my rescue."

The three of us look over his head and roll our eyes at one another. We are in so much trouble.

"What is scat?" Catherine asks.

"Oh, um, bear poop," he tells her. Which explains why he was looking at the ground.

Suddenly the front door crashes open with a bang, and Mick storms into the den with his gun drawn. His eyes are crazed and he's breathing hard. We shriek in terror and run behind the recliner until we realize who it is. Our ranger tries to stand up, but collapses back into the recliner. He's either frozen with fear or he's fainted.

Mick comes to a dead stop and looks around. No one moves while he slowly stares at each of us, and then his eyes drop to the ranger with the ice bag on his head.

We watch while he holsters his pistol and gives us "the look." Only this time I'm pretty darn sure I know what he'd like to do to us.

THIRTY

"Is this what I think it is?" Mick asks in a quiet voice.

"Depends, what do you think it is?" I ask softly.

Mick walks over to the bar, pulls out the whiskey decanter, pours a double shot, and drinks it. He refills his shot glass, turns around, and glares at us.

"Would someone like to tell me what's going on?" the ranger pleads.

"Yes, please tell us what's going on," Mick urges with a deadly smile.

On the one hand I knew this question was coming, and I was dreading it, but on the other hand I'm glad the ranger is alive and talking.

Cynthia walks between Mick and the ranger, wringing her hands.

"It's like this. We were all reading in the den when I looked up and saw a man sneaking around the back woods. He was acting strange, darting in and out of the trees, so naturally we thought it was Dusty. That's when we tried to call you, Mick, but all we got was your voice mail. The guy was getting closer and closer to the house, so we *had* to do something to defend ourselves. That's when Constance came up with a plan."

Mick crosses his arms and raises his eyebrows. "Imagine that, Constance coming up with a plan. Go figure," he says sarcastically.

"Well, yes," Cynthia continues. "She found two slingshots in the game room downstairs, so she and I hid behind the hot tub, and we told Catherine to run hide in the water garage with the Moomba, and when, um…the guy got closer, we sorta…um, well, started shooting him with…um, frozen mini bagels."

Her voice is barely a whisper. "The guy helped us by running into a tree, knocking himself out, and well, when we got to him, we realized he wasn't Dusty, but, um…this ranger." Cynthia stops and hangs her head.

"Wait a minute." The ranger stands up and gasps. "It was you ladies who attacked me and not some lamebrain kids? And with frozen mini bagels? Why did you do that?"

Mick runs his hands over his face and then goes up to the bar, pours another shot of whiskey, and gives it to the ranger.

"Here. Sit down and drink this. You'll need it while we explain everything."

Mick sits on the sofa and pats the seat next to him. "Ladies, why don't we all sit down."

The three of us walk over together and sit on the couch in unison. I think we're figuring there's safety in numbers. Good thing the couch is big.

Mick looks over at us and puts a hand up to his mouth. I'm not sure, but I think he's hiding a grin and I'm a little relieved.

Our ranger sits down in the recliner and puts the ice bag back on his head.

Mick clears his throat. "First, let me introduce myself and these ladies. I'm Mick Carelli, a private investigator. I was hired to be a bodyguard for Catherine, the lady sitting here in the middle. She's a syndicated columnist for the *Denver Advocate,* and she wrote an expose on the Mafia and their connections with the Colombian drug cartel. That pissed the Mafia off and they put a contract out on her. She came up here to hide out for a few weeks with her two friends, Cynthia and Constance."

Our ranger takes the ice bag off his head and knocks the shot of whiskey back in one gulp. "The Mafia, huh? Go on."

"We know the hit man, a guy named Dusty Galucci, was in town a few days ago looking for Catherine. I'm trying to verify if he's still around, but needless to say, we're all a little nervous right now."

Mick reaches over and squeezes my knee. I freeze and my eyes widen.

"The ladies get a little paranoid when anything unusual happens, like seeing a stranger wandering around the woods in their backyard. Unfortunately, you were in the wrong place at the wrong time, and these little women firmly believe in shooting first and asking questions later. I know myself what it's like to be on the receiving end of their hysteria. When I came to town, they thought I was Dusty, and this little thing right here knocked me out of a tour boat into the lake with her purse."

Our ranger chuckles. "That must've been some wallop."

Mick smiles. "Oh, it was. I left them alone this afternoon with instructions to stay in the house. Something they have a hard time doing." He cuts his eyes over at me and squeezes my knee a little harder.

"I told them to call me on my cell if they needed me, and they tried, but I guess I was in a dead spot and they couldn't get through. However, they did leave a message. A spine-tingling…chilling message that made my blood run cold, and then they didn't answer when I tried to call back."

This time Mick glares at Cynthia, and I can see her flinch out of the corner of my eye.

"That's the most amazing story I think I've ever heard," our ranger says, shaking his head. "I guess I'm lucky to be alive." He looks at Mick. "I guess we've both had a helluva afternoon."

That does it. I jump up and face the two men.

"Excuse me? *You've* had a helluva afternoon? What about us?"

I wave my arms and stomp around in circles. "Do you know what's it like to look out the window and see some strange man lurking around in your backyard? Knowing it could be a hit man? Oh, sure, we've got a state-of-the-art alarm system, but a lot of good that does if Dusty decides to shoot the back door out and go after us! We'd be sitting ducks—we wouldn't have a chance."

I'm on a roll. I lean over and poke Mick in the chest. "And where were you when we needed you, Mr. Carelli? In Grand Lake Village, that's where. We couldn't even get you on your cell! So we did the only thing we could think of to defend Catherine and ourselves. We came up with a plan, and by God, it was a good plan because if that guy *had* been Dusty, he'd be sitting here right now in that chair, tied up, with a knot on his head, instead of this ranger."

Everyone is quiet. They're staring at me with big, wide eyes. Mick rubs his chin and stands up. He goes behind the bar and pulls out three martini glasses and some lemons.

"I think someone needs a Lemon Drop Martini," he says.

THIRTY-ONE

I'm exhausted, and I've run out of steam. Then I remember the ranger. I turn to him.

"I'm sorry we attacked you with mini bagels this afternoon. We don't even know your name, Mr. Ranger, sir."

He smiles and hands me the ice bag. "It's Eli. Eli Patterson."

"I'm Constance, this is Cynthia, and you know which one Catherine is."

"It's a pleasure to meet such a spunky bunch of ladies. I'm sorry I caused you so much trouble today. Sometimes I get engrossed in what I'm doing, and I don't realize I may be trespassing on private property."

For the first time I take a good look at our ranger. If you ignore the big lump on his head, he's a great-looking guy. He's about sixty-ish, tall and slender and doesn't look a thing like Dusty. And he hasn't been able to take his eyes off Catherine all afternoon.

"Did you hike here from the trail?" Catherine asks him.

"Yes. I parked my Jeep at the Rainbow Bridge lot and hiked in."

"You're in no shape to hike back this evening," I tell him. "Please stay for dinner, and spend the night. We have extra bedrooms, and we can take you to the parking lot tomorrow morning."

"Oh, I don't want to impose."

"Trust me, you're no imposition. You'd make us all feel a lot better if you'd stay. It's the least we can do."

"Well, okay. Thanks."

"Can I get you an Advil or Tylenol for your head?" Catherine asks.

"Sure," Eli says, following her into the kitchen.

Cynthia and I walk over to the bar and sit down. Mick hands us each a martini and comes around and sits by me with his whiskey.

"Are you okay?" he asks me.

"I am now," I tell him, sipping my martini.

He sighs. "I'm sorry I've been so hard on you. And I hate to poke holes in your story, like if that had been Dusty out there this afternoon, he wouldn't have run away. He would've turned and shot at you, possibly injuring or killing you and Cynthia. But you were right about one thing. I shouldn't have left you to fend for yourselves, and I won't do it again."

I raise my eyebrows and give him "the look." Which is equal to a *Fifty Shades* smirk.

Cynthia giggles. "I don't know, Mick. Frozen mini bagels are pretty lethal. I think we could've brought Dusty down with them."

Mick chuckles. "You three are spunky ladies. How did you think of frozen mini bagels?"

Now I start giggling. "I don't know. I found the slingshots in the game room downstairs and I knew we'd need ammunition.

The only thing I could think of was the mini bagels in the freezer."

Cynthia goes from a giggle to a full-blown laugh. "You should have seen us huddled behind the hot tub. Constance called me Tonto, and I called her Kemo Sabe."

Catherine and Eli join us at the bar and Mick hands Catherine her martini.

"We were so upset when we discovered we'd knocked out a ranger," Catherine joins in. "Constance said we were three for three for bringing down the wrong guy."

Mick shakes his head. "You took about ten years off my life with that voice message. I could hear the panic in your voice, and when I called back and couldn't get anyone on the phone, I feared the worst. All I could hope was that you found a place to hide in the house and I'd get here in time to stop Dusty."

That sobers us up and we stop laughing.

I finish my martini and stand. "Let's go find something for dinner," I tell Cynthia as I head toward the kitchen. "Maybe some big, juicy steaks, baked potatoes, salad, garlic bread, and something for dessert. Yes! We definitely need something for dessert—something with chocolate. Lots and lots of decadent chocolate."

Mick jumps up too. "That's a great idea. I'm starving, and I can help with the grilling."

I turn around and point to the bar. "You can help by making three more Lemon Drop Martinis, please. Then we'll put you on grill duty."

135

"How about if I make a double chocolate cheesecake?" Cynthia asks. "I think we have all the ingredients, and I saw some fresh raspberries in the fridge to go with it."

I grab my heart. "Oh, don't toy with me, Cynthia."

Catherine comes up and locks arms with me and Cynthia. "I'll help in the kitchen," she tells everyone. Then she leans over and whispers to us. "Eli is single. What do ya think about that?"

We high five, low five, wiggle our butts, and boogie into the kitchen. We are so mature.

THIRTY-TWO

The next morning I get up, shower, and dress before I go down to the kitchen. I'm glad yesterday ended on a happy note. No bullet holes in the house, no dead bodies in the woods, no police drinking our coffee or putting yellow crime scene tape across the door. Instead we're a cheerful group eating dinner, playing cards, and chatting amicably. Any day that ends with Mick chatting amicably is a good day.

Coffee is made and I grab a cup before joining Eli and Mick on the front patio. The sun is coming up over Mount Baldy, and the lake is peaceful. Another gorgeous day in paradise.

"What? No breakfast ready?" I tease Mick.

He looks up and gives me the once-over before he grins. "Biscuits, sausage, and bacon are in the microwave."

"Hmm," I grunt. "You never disappoint."

"I aim to please."

The door opens and Catherine and Cynthia join us. Is it my imagination, or did Eli's face light up like a Christmas tree when he saw Catherine? I look at the goofy grin on his face. Nope, not my imagination. I look at Catherine. Same goofy grin. Hmmm, I believe Catherine and Eli were the last to go to bed. Now, which bed did they end up in?

"So, how did you sleep?" I ask Eli.

"Like a log."

Like a log, I bet! I almost snort, but instead smile and sip my coffee. Bet he doesn't have a headache this morning!

Mick is watching me and raises his eyebrows when I look his way. I raise my eyebrows in answer to his raised eyebrows. He raises his eyebrows higher and tips his head in answer to my raised eyebrows. I raise my eyebrows higher, and then wonder if I should bite my lower lip. Nah, that only works in *Fifty Shades*. Instead I cross my eyes and take a big gulp of coffee.

Mick chokes on his coffee and everyone looks his way. Now I raise my eyebrows in concern. I'm beyond bad this morning.

"So, what time do we need to leave for Granby?" Mick asks me.

I look at my watch. "In about an hour. We need to be at our appointment by ten. We'll swing around and drop Eli off at the parking lot first, and then head for the marina."

Everyone hustles into the house for breakfast, and an hour later we're in the Moomba heading for Rainbow Bridge.

We drop Eli off, after he and Catherine make a date for that night and exchange phone numbers. Mick looks at me and raises his eyebrows. I raise my eyebrows and roll my eyes. He shakes his head and smiles. I think we've discovered a whole new way to communicate— along with Braille and American Sign Language, we now have Eyebrow Raising.

We park the Moomba at the marina and walk to Cynthia's car. We're getting in when

Mick's cell phone rings. He answers it, says a few yeahs and okays, and hangs up.

"That was Sampson," he tells us. "Word on the street is Dusty is in Grand Lake Village."

"Dang! That's not what I wanted to hear," Catherine mutters.

We're all quiet for a few minutes and then Mick breaks the silence. "Do you mind driving by the police station so I can check on my Harley?"

"Sure," Cynthia agrees.

"Nice bike," I tell him when we see the Harley in the parking lot a few minutes later. "Really big, though."

"Have you ever ridden on a Harley?" he asks me.

"No, I've never been on any motorcycle, but it's on my bucket list."

"Maybe I can take you for a nice ride in the mountains after this mess with Dusty is over."

I look at him and raise my eyebrows. Yeah, right. I'm thinking what he'd really like to do is bounce me off on some remote mountaintop and leave me in the dust. Nice ride—my butt!

Mike grins and changes the subject. "So, tell me about this Flavia."

"She's young, beautiful, has a Russell Terrier dog, and moved here from New Orleans with her boyfriend two years ago," I tell him. "I think she's for real, and she speaks Cajun French."

"How did you find her?" he asks.

"I found her name and phone number on the town bulletin board when we got here," Cynthia tells him.

"Hmph," Mick grunts. He turns and looks at me and I'm expecting him to raise his eyebrows, but this time he just stares.

Wait a minute. How did he end up in the backseat with me?

THIRTY-THREE

We arrive at Flavia's at ten sharp. Like before, the front door opens before we can knock, and Flavia greets us.

"Right on time, and I'm ready," she tells us. "Oh, you're the mystery guest I saw in my tarot cards this morning." She looks at Mick and frowns. "But I didn't pick up that you'd be a man."

Today Flavia is dressed in a white peasant blouse, black leggings, and black ballet slippers. Her hair is pulled back into a long braid, and once again her arms are loaded with bangles and her neck is covered in strings of silver chains. She looks absolutely adorable.

Mick is looking at Flavia, and I introduce him.

"Flavia, this is Mick Carelli, Catherine's bodyguard," I tell her. "You remember the man I saw in my vision when we were here before? It wasn't Dusty, it was Mick."

Flavia reaches out and shakes Mick's hand. "Oh," she says in surprise, then smiles. "It's nice to meet you. May I call you Mick?"

"Please do."

"We brought back your disguises," Cynthia tells Flavia as she hands over a box. "They were a big help—thanks for letting us use them."

Flavia grins big and looks at Mick. "I'm glad I could help. I'm sorry about the confusion with your identity, Mick. Maybe I can help

Constance with her premonitions today, so they'll be more accurate. But I don't think she needs any help with her aim, that's for sure."

We all stop and stare at Flavia, speechless. What did she say about my aim?

Before anyone can say anything, Flavia's dog comes trotting into the room and sits by her feet. She reaches down and scratches his ears.

"This is Buddy. He's sweet and friendly, and I hope he won't bother anyone," she tells us.

Flavia straightens up. "I have everything set up in my breakfast nook in the back. Follow me and I'll tell you what I'd like to do."

Flavia and Buddy lead us down a small hallway that opens up into a bright, yellow kitchen. The breakfast nook next to it has bay windows, and five white chairs around an antique round table. Sunshine is streaming through the curtains, making the room cheery.

"Oh gosh, I was expecting something different," Catherine tells Flavia. "I thought we'd have to be in a dark room with the blinds down and the lights dimmed."

Flavia laughs. "I consider my powers and abilities to be good magic, not dark or evil. Plus, I'm not hiding any devices or phony contraptions to fool anyone. I don't lift tables or flicker lights, and I can't make apparitions appear. Or, at least not yet," she chuckles. "I want everything to be in the light and open. I think it makes my clients relax more too."

"Where do you want us to sit?" Cynthia asks.

"To start I'd like Constance and Catherine to sit next to me, and Mick, you and Cynthia can sit across from me."

We sit and Flavia continues. "The first thing I'd like to do is explain the tarot cards and the type of reading I'm going to use. Tarot cards are divided into what we call two arcanas, major and minor. The major arcana group represents the journey of humanity, and they are powerful cards named after gods and goddesses. The minor arcana is divided into four categories, cups, staves, swords, and pentacles. Cups represent love, life, inspiration, and pleasure. Staves represent creativity and expansion. Swords can transform painful situations into areas of personal growth. And pentacles can represent the harvest after the lessons."

Flavia stops. "Does anyone have any questions?" she asks.

We all shake our heads no.

"Okay then. We want to come to the table with open minds and willing hearts, so everyone take a deep breath and relax. I will do the reading for Catherine first. I'll shuffle the cards, Catherine will cut them, and then she'll knock on the deck three times, asking permission to enter into the psychic world of tarot."

Flavia turns to Catherine. "I'm going to do the past/present/future spread with you. You'll draw four cards from the deck. The first card represents the past, the second the present, the third the future, and the fourth is the expected outcome."

143

Flavia looks at Cynthia. "I'll do your reading next with the same spread."

Then she looks at me. "I'm not sure what I'm going to use with you yet. The same spread may be the best, but we'll see."

Flavia shuffles the cards, Catherine cuts the deck, and then Flavia places them on the table. She reaches over and knocks three times on the cards, and Catherine does the same. Flavia picks up the cards and fans them out. Catherine selects four cards and gives them to Flavia.

Flavia takes a deep breath and closes her eyes. Then she opens them and carefully turns the first card over.

We're all watching with intense interest, and I think I stopped breathing about five minutes ago.

THIRTY-FOUR

"This is your past card, Catherine, the eight of pentacles. This card tells me you're successful, creative, and a hard worker. You can easily lose yourself in your work, you're talented, and you're compensated well for what you do. You're passionate about your career. You're skilled and you have a lot of integrity and discipline."

Flavia stops and smiles. "All this makes sense to me because I know you're a brilliant writer and you love what you do. You feel blessed because you are paid well for your work, and you're content with your life. The seven pentacles above the woman in this card represent material rewards, which you are reaping. The pentacle on the ground is the last one the woman is creating. She's focused and inspired, and it symbolizes the circle of contentment in life. Catherine, you have created all this in your life and you're successful, but more importantly, you've achieved true happiness. Is this an accurate description of your past life?" Flavia asks Catherine.

"Yes. It's accurate and it's all true. Unbelievable." Catherine shakes her head.

Flavia picks up the next card. "This is your present card," she tells Catherine. "It's the seven of swords. This card tells me that you're feeling vulnerable and defenseless. You feel the need to protect and defend yourself. You'll notice that the woman in the card is trying to carry all the swords, but only five will fit in her arms, and she's looking behind her to make sure the two on the ground can't be used against her.

"Again, this card makes sense to me because the Mafia is threatening you," Flavia went on. "You have a contract on you, and you're trying to protect yourself by hiding out in Grand Lake Village. You're in new territory because you've never been in a position like this before and you're afraid. You don't know what to do to stop this madness, so you're trying to protect yourself the best way you can. Is this an accurate description of your present situation?"

Catherine nods her head yes.

"This card also tells me you need to be careful. You can't make any wrong steps or mistakes because the consequences will be harsh. Do you understand this, Catherine?"

Again Catherine nods her head yes.

Flavia picks up the next card and smiles. "Well, well. This is interesting. This is your future card, Catherine, and you chose the two of cups." Her smile widens and her eyes twinkle. "This card represents harmony, enchantment, and love. The two cups suggest the possibility of a nurturing relationship. You're going to meet someone and fall in love, Catherine. It may not be long-term, or lead to marriage, but it will be satisfying and fulfilling, and it will bring you much happiness."

"Oh my." Catherine smiles and looks at me and Cynthia. We nod at her knowingly.

I look at Mick. His face is expressionless and he's watching Flavia intently.

Flavia puts her fingers on the last card. "This is the outcome of your situation, Catherine."

She slowly turns the card over and I can see her breathe a sigh of relief.

"This is a major arcana card and it's very good news for you. It's the Star, the Goddess Inanna, and it means all will be well in your world. You'll be successful, have good fortune, and continue to be creative in your work. You can follow your dreams without fear or worry. But there is a caveat. All will be well in your world, but it may come with a price—an accident or injury, which could be slight or severe and cause you much pain. You need to remember the present card, Catherine. You can't let your guard down or become complacent. You must be careful."

Catherine swallows and nods her head. "I understand."

Flavia picks up all the cards and shuffles them. She looks across the table at Cynthia. "I'd like to do your reading next, Cynthia. Are you ready?"

Cynthia nods.

"Okay then. Can you and Catherine change places so you're sitting next to me, please?"

They exchange places at the table and Flavia hands the cards to Cynthia to cut. She does, and then they do the knocking and Flavia fans the cards out. Cynthia selects four.

Once again Flavia places the cards on the table, and reaches for the first one.

We all take a deep breath and watch her
turn the card over.

THIRTY-FIVE

"This is the three of swords, and it represents heartbreak and grief. A great loss in your life. This card has three swords piercing a heart, and that tells me you've had sharp pain and disappointment in the past. That you've had debilitating sorrow."

Flavia tenderly looks at Cynthia. "You don't have any children, do you, Cynthia?"

Cynthia shakes her head no and tears come to her eyes.

"You lost a child during pregnancy, and you've never been able to conceive again because of complications caused by that pregnancy, am I right?"

Cynthia nods her head.

Flavia reaches over and pats her hand. "You wanted to adopt, but your husband was against it, and that was another heartbreak in your life, is that true?"

Again Cynthia nods her head.

"Your dream of children and grand-children ended with that decision, and you've had to accept this loss in your life. And you did, with much strength and grace. This card tells me that although you experienced this great sadness, you and your husband have become close over the years. And you found strength, comfort, and support from those around you—mostly from Catherine and Constance. Is this a good description of your past, Cynthia?"

"Yes," Cynthia answers in a shaky voice.

"I'm sorry this is so painful. Sometimes readings can have disturbing parts. The cards can be revealing and upsetting, but I have to be truthful and tell you what I see and feel."

"I understand," Cynthia tells her. "You don't need to apologize. You warned us last time that we may hear things that aren't pleasant. Please, go on."

Wow! If I had any doubts about Flavia's abilities, I sure don't now. Catherine and I knew all about Cynthia's past, and her heartbreak of being childless, but hearing Flavia talk about it so intimately made me a true believer in her psychic abilities.

I sneak a peek at Mick. He's watching Flavia with eyes wide open.

Flavia reaches for the second card and turns it over.

"This is your present card, and it's the four of staves. This card represents stability in your home and marriage. You've put down deep roots and you're very satisfied. You're also a successful business owner, right?"

Cynthia nods her head yes.

"The card shows four staves planted on a grassy hill that are joined together with a garland and a couple standing underneath. This tells me you have a harmonious relationship with your husband and all is well in your world. Despite the sorrow from the past, you're happy with your present life. You and your husband celebrate not only the big things in life, but also the little things as well. Is this an accurate description of what's going on in your life right now, Cynthia?"

She nods her head, and Flavia reaches for the third card and slowly turns it over.

"This is your future card. It's the three of pentacles, but you'll notice the card is upside down, or reversed. This gives the card a different meaning. The three of pentacles is a building, or expansion card, but reversed it means you need to be careful about future expansions in your business. Were you thinking of expanding or moving your business, Cynthia?"

Cynthia nods her head and looks thoughtful. "I have been, yes. I own a hair and nail salon and was thinking about moving it to a new mall in our area."

"The appearance of this card doesn't mean you shouldn't do it. It just means that you may want to recheck your plans and make sure they're practical and appropriate for you right now. You may need to seek advice from someone who has more experience. This card tells me you need to take a reality check and make sure a move or expansion is right for you. Move forward with caution."

"Okay. That's good advice," Cynthia says with a smile.

Flavia puts her fingers on the last card and slowly turns it over. "This is your last card, the outcome of everything. Oh my, it's also a major arcana card—Judgment. It means there are going to be important decisions or news coming your way. This card tells me that you're approaching a major and necessary change in your life. It will be welcome, but it will also be frightening and a little bit scary. But you'll be up to the task and will be able to handle anything that comes your way with great confidence."

"Gosh, so much to think about," Cynthia says with a big sigh.

"Yes, tarot cards are meant to give direction and guidance in life. Not to necessarily predict the future. I hope these readings have been helpful to you, and to Catherine."

"Yes, but you know so much about us that we haven't told you. Did you get all that information from the tarot cards?" Catherine asks.

Flavia shakes her head. "No. The cards help me, but I have several psychic gifts. One is the ability to read auras, another is to see someone's past or present by their touch, and I'm also a medium."

Flavia turns to me. "And now it's your turn. Are you ready, Constance?"

I take a deep breath and nod.

THIRTY-SIX

Flavia shuffles the cards and I cut them. Then we both do the knocking thing and she fans them out.

"I'm going to do the same spread with you, so please select four cards," she tells me.

I select the cards and hand them to Flavia.

I'm nervous, but mainly because I'm not sure what little mystery in my life Flavia is going to expose to God, man, and Mick.

Flavia turns over the first card. "This is the prince of pentacles, and a powerful card. I sense that you're a strong, successful businesswoman. Knowledge and education have always been important to you. You're practical, dedicated, and grounded, and you're a hard worker. You're talented and quite the leader in your field. This is how you came to be promoted to a high position before you retired. Am I right?"

I nod my head, stunned she picked up on the fact that I'm retired.

Flavia turns the second card over. "This is your present card, the seven of staves." She stops and looks over at Mick and then back at me. "Well, how interesting. This tells me you're dealing with a difficult person in your life right now."

Catherine and Cynthia stifle their giggles, but Mick breaks out in a big smile. I roll my eyes and give them all "the look."

"You may continue to have some unpleasant experiences, but overall you'll be successful in reaching your goal," Flavia continues. "Hmm, and I sense a lot of…energy and intensity here. You're going through a challenging time in your life right now."

Catherine leans forward. "Is that *sexual* energy and intensity?" she asks.

I glare at Catherine and Flavia smiles and shakes her head. "I'd ask if this is a good explanation of what you're going through right now, Constance, but I think I already know the answer."

She turns the third card over. "This is a major arcana card—Beginnings. This is your future card, and it tells me you're going to be in a new adventure—a new phase in your life, possibly a promising relationship or a change at home. It's the start of a great, exciting journey. You may experience some fear, but you'll overcome it and come to appreciate this new stage of your life."

So far the future card sounds kinda nice. I could stand going through a new stage in my life, as long as it doesn't include a hit man trying to whack Catherine.

Flavia reaches for the fourth card and stops. She closes her eyes, moans, and slumps in her chair. We all sit up and look at one another. I'm not sure what to do.

I lean over and whisper, "Flavia? Are you okay?"

She moans again and starts mumbling. I put my ear to her lips. "I think she's doing that

Cajun French mumbo jumbo again," I tell the others.

"I'm Clarisse...Clarisse," I hear Flavia mutter softly. "I have found a worthy vessel for my gifts. A worthy vessel..." Her voice fades.

"Flavia! Are you okay?" I say a little louder.

I grab her hand.

Big mistake.

When my fingers touch hers, I feel a huge rush of energy leave her body and enter mine. I can't talk, breathe, or move, and I know I'm losing consciousness. In the mist of my fading vision, I see Catherine, Cynthia, and Mick rush over with worried faces, and I hear them call my name. Then, everything is black.

THIRTY-SEVEN

When I open my eyes, I see four faces staring at me. I'm lying on the couch in Flavia's den. She's sitting by me holding my hand, and Cynthia, Catherine, and Mick are hovering over my head.

"Wh-what happened?" I ask in a whisper. I try to sit up, but I fall back on the couch. I'm weak, and my body feels like jelly. My head is in a fog, and there's something heavy on my feet. I look down and see Buddy lying across them.

"You passed out," Flavia tells me. "Take a few deep breaths and see if you can sit up and drink a little of this water." She hands me a glass.

"But why did I pass out?"

A look passes between Flavia, Constance, Cynthia, and Mick. Uh-oh. I don't think I'm going to like the answer to that question.

I pull myself up to sitting and sip the water.

"How long was I out?"

"Too long," Mick answers. "Several minutes."

"So why do you think I passed out?"

Cynthia and Catherine pull up chairs close to me. Mick keeps standing and Flavia grabs my hand.

"I was telling your friends what I think happened. We'll know for sure now that you're awake."

I look at her, waiting.

"Constance, several months ago during a session, I encountered a strong presence or entity in the room with me and my clients. We were doing a séance, and I was connected with the spirit world. The presence I felt was an old soul who had crossed over to the other side many years ago. She joined our séance. I could feel and hear her, and she told me her name was Clarisse.

"Clarisse told me she was once a powerful psychic and wiccan. She had numerous paranormal gifts and she'd been looking for what she called a worthy vessel to pass her abilities to. She came into that séance and several others I held afterward, always mumbling about her worthy vessel and going from one person to another."

"Oookaaay. So what does that have to do with me?"

"When we were doing your reading, I suddenly felt Clarisse's presence, and then she took over my body. The next thing I remember is you touched me, and I felt Clarisse flow over to you. I came to, but you passed out. I believe Clarisse saw you as a worthy vessel for her paranormal gifts and used me to pass through you."

I'm in total shock. "A spirit named Clarisse passed through me and dropped off her paranormal gifts?" I ask in disbelief. "Like I'm a

FedEx drop-off box or something?" Then my eyes widen. "And how do I know if Clarisse only passed through? What if she's still inside of me?"

Flavia smiles gently. "I think you could feel her if she still possessed your body. Plus, I would know it, and from what I can see and feel, she's gone."

"Okay then. How do we know if she left her special gifts with me?"

"They'll show up. Probably very quickly. We'll do some tests in a minute, when you're up to it. But there's something else I should tell you about Clarisse. She's very different. All the spirits I've ever encountered would wait until they were called upon before they'd enter a séance, or they'd ask politely to be included, but Clarisse more or less barged in uninvited. She was quite a character, always sniffing around everyone to see if they were worthy of her gifts—very annoying, actually. I've never encountered any spirits like her before, or since."

I'm past shocked and heading for stunned. "I was possessed by a temperamental spirit? How did I get so freakin' lucky?"

"Umm, but that's not all. If Clarisse was as powerful as she claimed to be, she may have the ability to stay close by you—to watch over you, so to speak. So although she doesn't possess your body, she may be able to...visit you occasionally."

I fall back in the cushions of the couch. "Oh. My. God! Are you telling me I may be haunted by an obnoxious spirit, with an attitude no less, who has visiting privileges?"

Flavia sighs and pats my hand. "Yes, I am."

THIRTY-EIGHT

"That's just wonderful," I tell Flavia sarcastically. "I know my tarot cards predicted a new adventure in my future, but I was kinda hoping it was going to be something like a cruise down the Nile, or a hot-air balloon ride over the Napa Valley."

"I'm sorry, Constance. I don't know if Clarisse will bother you or not, but I wanted you to be prepared."

"So how do we find out if I got her gifts? And what kind of gifts do you think we're talking about here?"

"If you're up to it, let's find out."

I sit up and Buddy curls up next to me. Flavia watches us with a curious look on her face.

"What?" I ask her. "Is there something going on with Buddy? I like dogs, most animals, really."

"I'm not sure. Some Wiccans can attract animals to them to be used in their spells. Not as sacrifices, but to help make their spells more powerful. Buddy seems drawn to you more than usual, and if Clarisse had that power over animals, she may have passed it on to you."

"That's not so bad. I can handle that kind of gift."

"Hmmm…it may depend on how strong her power was. But let's see what else we can find."

Cynthia, Catherine, and Mick are watching me very, very closely. Too closely. They're making me a wee bit nervous.

"Okay, guys," I say. "I promise not to turn anyone into a toad, and I'm not going to jump on a broom and cackle. Can you back off a little and relax?"

"Cynthia, Catherine, I have some fresh lemonade in the kitchen," Flavia says. "Maybe you could get us all some?"

"Only if you have vodka to add to it," Cynthia tells her. "Just kidding. That's one of our inside jokes, you know. When life hands you lemons, make lemonade. And we add vodka to make it a Lemon Drop Martini. But sure, we'll go get us all some lemonade."

They tromp into the kitchen and Mick sits down in a chair close by me.

Flavia turns her attention back to me. "Okay, now close your eyes and concentrate and let's see what we can find out."

I close my eyes. "I'm ready."

"First, let's try telepathy. I'm thinking of an animal right now. Can you tell me which one?"

I concentrate and a giraffe comes to my mind. "Giraffe?" I ask.

"That's right! But that could be a lucky guess. Let's try another."

I keep my eyes closed and concentrate. "Aardvark?"

"Okay, right again, but let's try something harder. I'm thinking about an object in this room."

161

Yeah, that would be harder because I'm not familiar with her den. I concentrate and a *Sports Illustrated* magazine comes into my brain.

"This is strange, but I see a *Sports Illustrated* with a swimmer on the cover."

I open my eyes and from the look on Flavia's face, I know I'm right. "I guess that would be a yes?"

"Yes. Okay. I think you may have telepathy."

Cynthia and Catherine come in with our lemonade.

"She has telepathy?" Cynthia asks.

"Wow," Catherine exclaims. "What else?"

"We're still going through the list," I tell them as I gulp my lemonade. "What's next?" I ask.

"Well, we know you already have the power of precognition, or what you called premonitions, the perception of events or information before they occur. Let's try telekinesis. Concentrate on an object in this room, something simple, and see if you can move it. Try to move that *Sports Illustrated* magazine from the coffee table over to Mick."

I look at Mick. "Hmmm, well, if it's not the swimsuit edition, I don't think he'd be interested."

Mick's eyes widen. "Ha! Gotcha," I tell him. "Okay, now that I know which edition he wants, let me see if I can move it to him."

I concentrate and nothing happens. I concentrate harder, and a few seconds later a magazine moves out from under a stack and levitates slowly toward Mick. He grabs it out of the air, and stares at me.

I gasp. "Oh crap! Did I do that?"

"Oh yes! Mick, is that the swimsuit edition?" Flavia asks.

Mick nods his head yes.

"Okay then. Let's see if you can move something heavier. Try that candlestick on the table by the door," Flavia directs.

I look at the candlestick and concentrate hard. Nothing happens, so I concentrate even harder.

The candlestick slowly rises from the table, and suddenly my glass of lemonade is snatched out of my hand, glides across the room, and dumps over on Mick's head.

"Omigod! I didn't do that," I exclaim. "I swear—I didn't do that. I don't know how it happened."

I hear a wicked laugh, and Flavia turns to me with a gasp.

"Did you hear that laugh?" I ask her.

"Yes, I did—that's Clarisse!" Flavia cries. "She's here."

I turn back to Mick. "Clarisse did that, not me. You gotta believe me."

THIRTY-NINE

Flavia gets a towel for Mick, and he wipes off the lemonade. "I don't think Clarisse likes you," she tells him.

"So, that's what I'm gonna hear from now on?" he asks with a wee bit of sarcasm. Okay, a lot of sarcasm. "Instead of 'the devil made me do it,' I'm going to hear 'Clarisse made me do it'?"

"I'm sorry, Mick. But I promise you I was concentrating on the candlestick. I wasn't even paying attention to my glass of lemonade. Did you guys hear her laugh?" I ask.

Cynthia, Catherine, and Mick all shake their heads no.

"Flavia and I heard her. It was a loud, wicked laugh. So why do you think she did that?"

Flavia looks worried. "I think she's watching us to make sure her powers transferred to you okay. But I think she has another purpose, and it's not good."

"What?" Now it's my turn to look worried.

"I think she was testing to see if she could control any of her powers through you. You notice she didn't do anything when we were testing you for telepathy, but when we got into the telekinesis, that's when she did her little stunt."

"Ah, so when I'm doing telekinesis, she can do it too? Is that what you're telling me?"

"Yes, that's what I think is happening."

"Okay, then I probably shouldn't try to move things again, if that's the case."

"Not when she's around. And your gift as a medium will develop more as time goes on, so you'll be able to sense her presence."

"Omigod, Flavia! Are you telling me I have that gift too? In addition to the telepathy, precognition, and telekinesis? What's left?" I ask.

"Not too much."

I flop down on the couch. Cynthia and Catherine flop down with me.

"This is overwhelming." I sigh. "And you forgot about that animal attraction thing."

"Oh yeah, let's not forget about that," Cynthia adds. "We got our own Dr. Doolittle here."

"I'm that too?" I ask quietly. "Can I talk to the animals? Am I a Dr. Doolittle?"

Flavia shakes her head. "I'm not sure. I don't think you can talk to animals, but I don't know a lot about it. This will be an area you'll learn more about as time goes on, I guess."

"Wait a minute," Catherine exclaims. "Constance, if you have all this power, you can handle Dusty. Just think, you can read Dusty's thoughts, stop his bullets, or heck, you can sic Clarisse on him if he bothers us."

"And if that doesn't work," Cynthia adds, "you can sic all the animals on him."

"Okay. So, I gotta few questions, Flavia. Can I block out some of this stuff? You know. I don't always want to read someone's mind, or move objects, or see ghosts or foresee the future. Can I block it out?"

"Yes, you can. It's only when you concentrate on that precise ability or gift that you can do it. Except for the premonitions. You were never able to control those in the past, and I'm not sure what will happen now. And then there's Clarisse. I don't think you can stop her if she decides to pay you a visit."

"It's a relief I can at least control the telepathy and telekinesis. I don't want to be a freak, or anymore of a freak than I already am. And I certainly don't want my friends to think I'm spying on them."

"Oh, Constance! We would never think that, would we?" Cynthia asks.

"Not me, ever," Catherine confirms.

"I might," Mick grumbles.

"But what I worry about is Clarisse," Flavia tells me. "She may become a real nuisance in your life, and I don't know how to send her back to the other side. It takes a strong medium to do that, and I only know of one who has that much power."

"Who?" I ask.

"My older sister, Beignet. She lives in New Orleans and has a little shop in the French Quarter. She's the most powerful Wiccan in the South."

"So what would we need to do? Could we call her and see if she can send Clarisse back?"

"I'll get in touch with her, but I have a feeling you'll have to go to New Orleans and meet with her in person. I don't think this is something she can do over the phone or by Skype. And Beignet won't leave New Orleans."

"Maybe Clarisse won't be a problem. If I don't use any of her powers, maybe she'll get bored and go back on her own."

Flavia shakes her head. "I don't think she's going to be that easy, unfortunately. And I don't think you'll be able to ignore your powers either."

FORTY

Dusty spends all day Sunday in bed. On Monday afternoon he gets up and takes a shower, which proves to be irritating and difficult because of his cast. Room service brings him some trash bags, and he's able to wrap them around his cast to keep it dry while he showers, but it isn't easy. And dressing is a real challenge. After what seems like an eternity, he finally gets his shirt and pants on and is lounging on the small deck outside his room chain-smoking. His addicted body desperately needs a tobacco fix after going without for several days.

He sits in the mountain sunshine and thinks about his next move. Tomorrow he'll go into town and look around. Maybe check on renting a boat. If push comes to shove, he could call his uncle and have him send someone to help. But at least now he knows for sure which house the James woman is staying in.

Uncle Rocky had called him the day before to find out how he was doing. He made up something about tripping over a log while stalking the house and breaking his arm, but didn't go into detail about the wasps or ticks.

"Chris' almighty," Rocky had yelled. "How the hell are ya gonna shoot someone with your fuckin' arm in a cast?"

"I broke my left arm, and I'm right-handed, Uncle," Dusty had assured him.

"Hmph! Well, get the job done, and let me know if you need any help."

Dusty gets up and takes some of the pain pills they gave him at the hospital. Then he grabs his room key and heads for the restaurant downstairs. He'll chase the pills with a draft beer and get a bite to eat. And plan out his strategy to get this hit done so he can be home by July Fourth.

FORTY-ONE

I'm drained by the time we get back to Grand Lake Village. I think we're all were pretty much whipped. We stop for lunch at the Blue Water Bakery and find a shady spot on the outdoor patio to enjoy our sandwiches. Then Mick drives us back to the house in the Moomba, and I immediately crash for an afternoon nap.

When I get up several hours later, I'm refreshed and feeling much better. The house is quiet and peaceful. Mick and Cynthia are downstairs playing cards, and Catherine is in her room getting ready for her date with Eli.

"You look rested," Cynthia tells me when I enter the den.

"I feel tons better. Are you going with Catherine on her date tonight?" I ask Mick.

He smiles. "I'm thinking about it."

"Does she know you're thinking about it?"

His smile broadens. "She will."

I sit down at the table and watch the two of them anguish over their cards.

"What are they doing tonight, do you know?" I continue.

"I think they're going to the Rocky Mountain Repertory Theatre in Grand Lake to see *All Shook Up,*" Cynthia tells me.

"Talk about ironic. That could be our theme song right now."'

170

"Maybe we should all go," Mick suggests. "I hate to be a third wheel, but I can't let Catherine out of my sight."

I shake my head. "Now I know how the royals feel. How can you have an intimate night out when you have security and bodyguards breathing down your neck?"

"You can't," Cynthia answers. "And I don't know if we can get tickets for tonight. They're probably sold out."

"Well, how is Eli getting them?" I ask.

"I think he has connections."

"Maybe his connections can scare up three more for us," Mick says.

"Three more what?" Catherine asks as she comes in the room.

I sigh. "Tickets for tonight's show for me, Cynthia, and Mick. Mick doesn't want you to go without him."

"Oh, I figured that, and told Eli. He called me a little while ago and told me he was able to get tickets for all of us."

"Thank God you're okay with us tagging along. But if that's the case, I think I'll go take a shower and change my clothes— freshen up a little bit."

"Yeah, me too," says Cynthia. "Gin!"

Mick throws his cards down. "Damn! That's four straight hands you've won." He gets up and stretches. "I think I'll go outside and check around and make sure there's no sign of Dusty."

He leaves and Cynthia and I go upstairs to get ready. Less than an hour later, we're all on the back patio. The plan is to meet Eli at the theatre and then go out for a light dinner afterward.

We're sipping drinks and nibbling appetizers, killing a little time before we have to leave, when I notice all the cute, woodland creatures in our yard. Chipmunks and squirrels are darting through the leaves on the ground, birds are perched on tree limbs warbling their hearts out, and several deer are watching us from a safe distance. I'm not sure, but I think we have an overabundance of woodland creatures in our yard this evening. And now everyone else notices too.

"Holy crap! Look at all the animals back here," Catherine exclaims.

"Yes, I noticed too," Cynthia says. "Aww, look at those little field mice frolicking in the wood stack over there, and the birds chirping in the trees, and the mama duck and her babies coming onshore and heading toward us. Aren't they cute?"

"There wasn't this much wildlife here when I was out about an hour ago," Mick notes.

I look at all the happy little critters surrounding us. "Holy crap is right. I feel like I'm in a Disney movie," I blurt out.

"I think they're drawn to you, Ms. Doolittle, by your magical powers," Catherine giggles.

"Maybe we should go inside before Snow White draws too many of her friends," Mick suggests.

"It's about time for us to leave anyway," Catherine tells us.

We gather our stuff and go in.

We're grabbing jackets, caps, purses, and keys, and chatting and laughing when I turn to look out the back window. The porch is filled with squirrels, chipmunks, rabbits, birds, mice, ducks, and deer watching me through the glass. And double crap! I think I even see a skunk in the mix!

"Omigod! Look at all the animals."

"Holy Moses," Cynthia bursts out. "Constance, go out and see if you can get them to leave and go back to the forest."

"You think I can do that?" I ask.

"It's worth a try. See what happens when you go out and talk to them."

Why not? They'll either run away, stay put, or worst-case scenario, mob me.

I open the back door and gingerly step out. Some of the animals back up, but most stay still. They're all watching me with their dark, trusting eyes.

"Okay, you guys, go on home. Shoo! Go back to the forest or lake or wherever you came from," I coax them.

I turn and see everyone watching from the back window, and I shrug my shoulders. The critters are still looking at me.

"Really, go home! Go to your nests and dens and beds for the night, please! Go! Shoo!"

I wave my fingers at them and slowly, one by one, they turn and walk, scurry, waddle, and fly back to the woods. Soon, I'm the only one left on the porch. I turn and look at my friends in awe.

FORTY-TWO

The next morning I'm up at dawn. We had a wonderful time the night before. The show was terrific, and we were all in a fabulous mood when we went to dinner at Caroline's Cuisine, a wonderful four-star restaurant in Grand Lake. No one mentioned what happened to me that day, and the best thing was Clarisse didn't show up either. I'm hoping she stayed in Granby. If I'm lucky she's a directionally challenged ghost and will never find me.

After dinner we all piled in the Moomba, including Eli, and came back to the house for a nightcap and some cards. It was after one o'clock when I finally crawled into bed.

I'm not sure why I woke up so early, but I'm feeling melancholy and sad. I decide to watch the sunrise from the front patio, so I slip on a pair of jeans and a sweatshirt and head downstairs.

The house is quiet and I even beat Mick up. I make some coffee and grab a cup before I head out the front door.

There's nothing better to me than sitting by the lake, drinking a great cup of coffee and watching the rays of the morning sun slowly creep over Mount Baldy. The fish are jumping out of the water for their early-morning breakfast of gnats and mosquitoes, the mama ducks are quacking at their little ones, and the happy birds are chirping. It's a magical time on Grand Lake. The crisp mountain air is exhilarating and cold, and I'm glad I have on a warm sweatshirt and jacket.

In the peace of the morning, I think about all that's happened recently. In just one week I've gone from a semi-sorta-kinda-retired Grammy with an occasional paranormal experience, to a freaky woman with a bunch of psychic gifts that scare the crap out of me. And I can't forget about Clarisse, the psychotic witch-ghost who's decided to make me her new best friend.

I worry that this new development in my life may affect my friendship with Catherine and Cynthia. Who wants a BFF who can tap into your mind at any time, or has a demented ghost following her around who loves to play mean tricks and pranks on unsuspecting humans?

I sigh, and without thinking reach down and pet the little fawn that's nosing up to me. I'm caressing its silky head and looking at its adorable spots when reality hits me like a brick, and I jerk my hand back. I look around quickly to see how many critters have joined me, and fortunately there are only a few—and no skunks.

But that's another thing. I've turned into a modern-day Snow White. I love animals, but it blows my mind to know I'm attracting all sorts of wildlife, which could include lion and tigers and bears, oh my!

"Alright, everyone, go back to where you belong," I tell the little critters. "Go on now—shoo!"

The patio clears, and once again I'm by myself with my thoughts.

"You're up early this morning," Mick says from behind me.

I turn and muster up a smile. "Yeah, and now with all my magical, voodoo powers, I can tell if Dusty's around or not. I tried my telepathy when I came out to make sure he's not hiding in the woods, and he's not, so don't get mad at me for being out here by myself."

"From what I could see, you had plenty of company a few minutes ago."

I sigh. "Yes, my little woodland creatures came to pay me a visit. I sent them back home."

Mick comes around and sits in the chair next to me. He's dressed in jeans and a T-shirt and has on his leather jacket. His dark curly hair is slightly damp from his shower, and I can faintly detect a nice manly man smell coming from his direction.

"Are you okay this morning?" he asks.

"I guess. I'm thinking about all that's happened this past week. First, Catherine's article comes out and she gets in trouble with the Mafia and they put a contract out on her, and now I have all these paranormal gifts I didn't ask for, and a deranged ghost following me around. Oh, and by the way, I've turned off my telepathy, so your thoughts are safe from me."

Mick smiles. "I wasn't worried about that. You're an ethical and honest woman—not the type to intrude on anyone's thoughts unless you have a good reason."

"Yeah, but would you want to be best friends with someone like me right now? I feel

177

like a real weirdo. My whole life is out of control."

"Is that what's worrying you? You're afraid Catherine and Cynthia won't want to be around you, or be friends with you anymore? From what I've seen these past few days, it'd take more than a few paranormal powers and a crazy ghost to keep them away. You three have a deep, loyal friendship."

"You think so? Yes, I guess I'm worrying about keeping my friends, or even making new ones. Word gets around fast when you're different. I learned a long time ago to keep my premonitions a secret. People think you're a freak or unbalanced if you go around warning them about things that are about to happen. Catherine has always been a true friend, and then Cynthia came along and joined in with us, and we've been inseparable ever since. I'm really lucky."

Mick reaches over and takes my cup, then stands up.

"Time for a refill and for you to stop worrying. Catherine and Cynthia will never stop being your friend. And as for making new friends, I'd sure like to be one. In fact, I'd like to be more than a friend, if you catch my drift."

I look at him surprised. "Are you kidding? You'd go out with someone like me? And after everything I did to you?"

Mick grins. "When this is all over, I'd like very much to go out with you," he reaches over and squeezes my shoulder. "You're an amazing woman, Constance. Now relax, and I'll bring you another cup of coffee."

I don't know what to say, so I do what I normally do. I shut up.

FORTY-THREE

"What's on the agenda for today?" Mick asks when everyone has joined us on the patio.

"Well, we haven't hiked Adams Falls yet. We could do that," I suggest.

"Ummm, sounds good to me," Cynthia agrees.

"Are you working today, Eli?" I ask.

"Yes, but I'll be off tomorrow and Thursday, the fourth."

"Oh, that's right, Thursday is July Fourth. I almost forgot about it with everything that's been going on. Usually this house is packed for the Fourth, but this year Rachel and Sam took their whole family on a Disney cruise to the Caribbean. They won't be back until next week, and my kids and grandkids are waiting to come up this weekend."

"I think we'll have a packed house for the Fourth after all," Cynthia tells us. "Dave e-mailed me last night and he's coming home early. He should get in tonight and he's going to drive up tomorrow. I hope that's okay, but I figure there's always room for one more."

"Of course it's okay! And Eli, you're welcome to crash at the house with us if you don't have any plans for the holiday." I'm excited and anticipating a fun week. "It'll be great to have a full house. We have so much we can do—waterskiing, kayaking, and biking— and we have a perfect spot on the front patio to watch the July Fourth fireworks over the lake."

"I'd love to stay here, if it's okay with everyone," Eli says. "And if Catherine doesn't mind."

Catherine's face lights up. "I don't mind at all."

"I think I'll pass on the kayaking," Mick tells us quickly.

That gets a hoot and a high five from us, and suddenly my melancholy mood has lifted.

We hear a boat approaching, and when it gets close, I recognize the couple who keep the house clean and filled with groceries.

"It's Lola and Pete," I tell everyone. "The caretakers for Bootie's Hideaway. What perfect timing! They probably brought groceries and will help us clean up the place. We can make a grocery store run before we come back this afternoon to make sure we have everything we need for the Fourth."

When the boat docks, we all help unload bags of groceries, and I introduce Lola and Pete to everyone.

"Holy schnikes! I'm not sure they left any food in Grand Lake for us to buy," Cynthia exclaims when we're unpacking the bags in the kitchen. "They brought so much. I want to pay for my share, how do I do it?"

"You can't," I tell her. "Rachel and Sam appreciate family and friends coming up and using the place. If we didn't, they'd have to pay Lola and Pete to come more often. You can't leave a vacation home empty for too long, or things go wrong, like plumbing or critters getting in places they shouldn't. If you want to

181

do something for them, you can write in their logbook. They love for people to leave messages and tell about their experiences while they're up here."

"Oh good Lord," Catherine pips in. "There's no way we can write all our experiences in their logbook! Can you imagine how it would sound?"

She leans over, grabs a banana from the fruit bowl, and holds it up like a microphone. Then mimics in her best Katie Couric voice, "It's day one and we arrive at the peaceful mountain village of Grand Lake to escape the stress of city life, and to hide from an assassin who's been hired to whack Catherine. So far, so good, Catherine's still alive, and there's no sign of the hit man."

Cynthia and I are cracking up while we watch Catherine, ace correspondent, continue to do her thing.

"Day two—we spend the day shopping in Grand Lake Village and spying on a man we think was sent to take out Catherine. We break into his room at the Sagebrush and later knock him into the lake before we discover he's one of the good guys and sent to be Catherine's new bodyguard. All ends well, as Catherine is still alive and the bodyguard decides not to sue."

"Oh wait, I've got one," Cynthia exclaims, and grabs the banana. "But I gotta be Savannah Guthrie. How's this?" She puts the banana in front of her mouth. "Day three—after a wonderful boat ride on Shadow Mountain Lake and a picnic on one of the islands, we end the day kayaking along the shores of Grand Lake and inciting a duck riot. The ducks attack the bodyguard and overturn his kayak. However, everything turns out okay, because no ducks were hurt and the bodyguard doesn't drown."

"Oh, I gotta get in on this," I laugh and it's my turn to get the banana. "Only, can I be Meredith Vieira? I just love her." I clear my throat and talk into the banana. "Day four—we spend the day relaxing and reading until we see a strange man snooping around the backyard. We think it's the hit man and we attack him with slingshots and frozen bagels, only to learn we maimed one of our friendly forest rangers. He survives, decides not to press charges, and starts dating Catherine."

Catherine is laughing hard, and the banana is back to her. "Day five—we meet with a psychic in Granby who reads our tarot cards and unwittingly becomes a transmitter for a wacko ghost who picks Constance to receive her precious gifts of telepathy, telekinesis, and trouble, and dang if she doesn't dump them all on her."

"Yep, just your normal, everyday tourist adventures," Cynthia says. "And we didn't mention the Dr. Doolittle animal-attraction thing."

"Oh, let's not go there," I beg. "And let's all agree that writing in the logbook is *not* a good idea."

Mick pokes his head through the kitchen door. "Eli needs to get back to Grand Lake. Are you ladies about through?"

"Why don't you take him while we help put all this up," Cynthia suggests. "When you get back, we'll be ready to go on that hike."

Mick raises his eyebrows and folds his arms across his chest. "No way. I haven't forgotten what happened the last time I left you three alone. And I promised I'd never do that again."

"You ladies go on," Lola urges, coming into the kitchen. "I can do this. We plan to spend the day here, so I have plenty of time."

"Okay then, you don't have to tell us twice. Thanks, Lola!" I give her a quick hug before we all bounce out the front door.

We pile into the Moomba and head for Grand Lake. Twenty minutes later we're on the boardwalk outside the marina.

"I'm starving, and no wonder! Mick didn't make our breakfast this morning," Catherine teases.

"Why don't we have breakfast at the Sagebrush?" I suggest. "You've got us all spoiled, Mick, but how about if we treat you this morning?"

"Fine by me. I can handle breakfast with three beautiful ladies."

"Well, we'll see if we can find three for you," Cynthia tells him with a straight face.

"Okay, if you can find three who won't dunk me in the lake or pour lemonade on my head."

Eli grins and shakes his head. "Or that won't ambush me with frozen mini bagels."

We laugh and tease one another all the way to the Sagebrush, and after a short wait, we're seated in a large booth. We give the waitress our orders and start talking about our upcoming hike.

"So, how long is this hike?" Mick asks.

"If you only hike to the falls, it's not long," Eli tells him. "But if you want a longer hike, you can take the East Inlet Trail. That's about eleven miles."

"It's a beautiful trail, and we can always turn back if we get tired," I tell everyone.

"I'll try to keep up, but I'm not much of a hiker," Mick warns us. "Most of my exercise is done in a gym or on my Harley. However, I think I've lost about ten pounds this week trying to keep up with you three, with all the walking, shopping, and kayaking I've done. Not to mention the swimming!"

FORTY-FOUR

Dusty is at the Sagebrush Restaurant, scrunched down in the booth next to Catherine and her friends. He couldn't believe his good luck when he saw them come into the restaurant, and then watched as the waitress led them to the booth right next to his.

While they laugh and talk, he eats and listens to them make plans to go on a hike. He scowls when he hears the word *hike*, but then a lightbulb goes off in his brain. And being Dusty, naturally it's a low-watt bulb. He decides he'll follow them, and when they get to a remote area on the trail, he'll hide behind a rock or tree and take down the James bitch and her two friends. Then he'll disappear in the forest before anyone figures out what's happened.

He frowns. It's not the best plan in the world. He'll have to make sure he escapes quickly and no one sees him. But it sure beats trying to hike back to that secluded house she's staying in. And going by boat is too risky. He took the Grand Lake tour that morning and was able to spot the house even without his binoculars. From what he could tell, there was no good place to pull a boat up to the shore without being seen.

He's not happy about going on another hike, but this time it'll be different. This time he knows what to expect, and he'll be successful because he's got the perfect hiding place for his pistol—his sling!

Dusty slurps down his coffee, lays a twenty-dollar bill on the table, and slips out of the booth. He walks to his parked car, looks around to make sure no one is watching, then opens the glove box and takes his pistol out and hides it in his sling. He walks back to the park across the street from the Sagebrush, and chain-smokes while he watches the door.

FORTY-FIVE

After we finish breakfast and say our good-byes to Eli, we're on our way to the marina parking lot to pick up Cynthia's car when I get a strange feeling—like someone's watching us. I turn and look behind me but don't see anything unusual. Well, nothing more unusual than being on the boardwalk in Grand Lake Village two days before the Fourth of July with about a billion other people.

"What's up?" Mick asks me. "You keep looking behind you. Did you see someone, or...hear anything?"

"By 'hear anything,' do you mean have I turned on my voodoo-spooky telepathy?"

"Yeah, that."

"No, but maybe I should. I have the strangest feeling we're being followed."

"There's a bench in front of that ice-cream shop," Cynthia says. "Let's stop there for a few minutes."

I plop down on the bench and Catherine heads for the door of the shop. "Maybe I should hide out in here in case Dusty is close by. I should probably buy some ice cream too."

"Good idea, and I think I'll join you," Cynthia agrees.

Mick grins. "I'll keep watch out here with Constance while you two hide out in the ice-cream shop where it's safe."

I smile and shake my head, then close my eyes and concentrate. I'm not exactly sure what to do, so I wing it, and in seconds I start hearing voices in my head. Lots and lots of voices are coming at me from every direction, some soft and some loud. I recognize Mick's thoughts, and he's wondering if they have chocolate chip ice cream.

"Yes, they do," I tell him softly without opening my eyes.

I hear him laugh and then he sits down next to me and grabs my hand. Suddenly I'm bombarded with his thoughts of kisses and touches and caresses, and yowzer! It turns X-rated real fast, and that's when I know he's playing with me, so I open my eyes and give him "the look."

"Cut it out, Carelli. I'm trying to be serious here."

He's smiling really big. "I am too."

I pull my hand away from his and concentrate again. "Jeez, this is crazy! The women are worried about keeping up with their kids and if they look fat in shorts, and the men are wondering what the hotties look like without any clothes on," I tell him. "I don't hear anything threatening, or Catherine's name in any of the thoughts, so I don't think Dusty is near. Unless he's one of the men thinking about the hotties."

"I'll go in and get Cynthia and Catherine," Mick tells me.

"Wait a minute! I'm going inside too. I may need some ice cream after all this mental work."

We go in and spot Cynthia and Catherine sitting at one of the small tables with double-scoop ice-cream cones.

Mick gets in the line at the counter. "What kind of ice cream do you want?" he asks.

"Same as you, double chocolate chip."

He raises an eyebrow. "Can you tell what I'm thinking now?"

I look at him innocently. "No, I turned off my telepathy."

"Good thing."

I grin and go over to Cynthia and Catherine.

"Did ya find out anything?" Catherine asks me when I sit down next to them.

"Only that there's a boatload of insecure women in this world who worry if their pants make their butts look big, and men who can't stop thinking about all the women's butts."

"Go figure," Cynthia says.

"I didn't hear anything about you, Catherine, or any random thoughts of violence, thank God. I guess I'm getting paranoid in my old age."

Mick comes to the table with two double-scoop ice-cream cones and hands me one.

Before I can even lick it, the cone is snatched out of my hand, and I hear that all-too-familiar cackle in my ear.

"Oh no! She's back! Clarisse is here," I warn everyone.

Catherine and Cynthia are no longer holding their cones, but watching them float up in the air to join mine. We stare in awe as cone after cone in the shop rises to the ceiling while the tourists look around in confusion.

"Quick! Let's get out of here," I whisper loudly.

We rush out with Mick in the rear, and all the ice-cream cones following close behind him. Mick slams the door, and we hear a dozen ice-cream cones hit the glass with a loud splat!

"Crap! That was close," Cynthia exclaims. "I think Clarisse was after you again, Mick."

"Ya think?" he quips sarcastically while we power walk to the marina.

"What a waste of good ice cream. That crazy ghost needs to get a reality check," Catherine moans.

"Oh, yeah, I'm sure that's her number one concern right now." It's my turn to be sarcastic. "That's gotta be right up there with—does this dress make my ectoplasm butt look big?"

FORTY-SIX

"Jeez! Can a ghost be bipolar?" Cynthia asks when we're in her car on our way to the trail parking lot.

"We'll have to ask Flavia the next time we see her," Catherine answers. "But I think that ghost-witch definitely has some mental issues."

"She certainly has something against men," Mick comments. "Maybe she was scorned by a lover or was in a bad marriage in her past life."

"I'm wondering now if it was Clarisse I was sensing when we left the Sagebrush," I tell everyone. "And back there at the ice-cream shop, I wasn't trying to do any telekinesis, only telepathy. I'm thinking Clarisse can piggyback onto any of her gifts whenever I'm doing anything paranormal. I can sorta control when I'm doing the telepathy and telekinesis, which will keep her away, but I'm not sure about the premonitions. I never could control when I had one of those."

"'Sorta' control?" Mick asks me suspiciously.

I sigh. "With the telepathy I have to make sure I don't let my guard down, or I'll accidentally start listening to everyone's thoughts. I don't have to concentrate hard to do it, like I do with the telekinesis. I dunno, maybe these paranormal gifts are starting to grow on me. I think they're getting stronger every day, which is alarming because that could mean

Clarisse might be making more visits. I don't know what to expect anymore."

"Don't worry about it," Mick tells me and pats my hand. "We'll figure out how to handle Clarisse as time goes on."

"Mick's right," Cynthia says. "Look how we were able to sidestep her at the ice-cream shop. That could've been real ugly if you hadn't urged us to get out when we did."

"That's true," I agree. "And anyway we should be concentrating on Dusty. He's the real danger as far as I'm concerned, and much more dangerous than Clarisse."

"Yes, so far all Clarisse does is juvenile, practical jokes against me, and I can take it." Mick grins. "I'm a big boy."

We arrive at the parking lot and grab our gear and get out. We all have little backpacks with water, trail mix, cell phones, cameras, ChapStick, and of course, our wallets and credit cards. God forbid we would go on a hike without a MasterCard or Visa in our pockets.

There are crowds of tourists all along the trail going up to Adams Falls. We have to wait in a little line to look at the beautiful waterfall as we circle around the rocks overlooking the rushing stream. It's slow going, but when we turn off on the East Inlet Trail, the crowds thin and we're able to hike at a faster pace.

"What a gorgeous day, and what a gorgeous trail," Catherine exclaims.

"It's so pure and pristine up here," Cynthia notes. "This mountain air is exhilarating and the scent of the pines is wonderful. I've almost completely forgotten about Clarisse. Do you think she followed us up here?"

"It's hard to tell, but I bet if I try anything paranormal, she'd be on us like a tick on a dog," I answer.

"Yep, so don't concentrate on anything but hiking," Catherine tells me. "We can't afford for her to show up and harass Mick when she's got rocks and tree branches to throw at him."

"Good point," Mick agrees.

We hike for about an hour, and then stop to take a break on some big rocks.

"Not too many people on this trail today," Mick notes. "Most of the tourists stayed back around Adams Falls."

"That's an easy hike with the big reward of seeing the falls at the end, so it's popular. But once you get off on this trail, it becomes more challenging. There's a little path off to the left up ahead that meanders back to the main trail and the falls. It's not a well-known trail, but it has some breathtaking scenery. Would you all like to go that way, or would you prefer staying on this main trail for awhile longer before we track back?" I ask.

"Why don't we take the little path? That sounds like fun if it's okay with Catherine and Mick," Cynthia says.

"Fine by me," Mick says.

"Me too," Catherine agrees.

"Okay then. I think it's right around that curve. It's only about a two-hour hike back to the car from here, and that should get us back to the house by four or five."

"You're the leader of the pack, so lead on, Kemo Sabe," Cynthia tells me.

I roll my eyes, grab my pack, and head toward the cutoff.

FORTY-SEVEN

Dusty is watching the group ahead of him relax on several large rocks. He's out of breath, but so far he's managed to keep up with them. He's sitting on a log behind some trees, out of their line of sight, watching them laugh and talk. He slowly removes his pistol from its hiding place and checks the safety. He's almost close enough to take a shot, but decides he's still too far away. He doesn't want to take any chances on missing the James bitch. He gets up to sneak in closer when he notices the group is up and moving down the trail.

"Shit," he mutters under his breath as he quickly puts his pistol back in his sling.

He follows at a safe distance, and when the group disappears around a curve, he picks up his pace. Once again he's wearing the wrong clothes for hiking. His leather shoes slip and slide on the rocks, and his cast is itching like crazy. He's sweating like a pig and his dress shirt is sticking to him like glue. He's thinking that maybe he should stop, find a good spot to hide, and wait for them to turn around and come back. That idea is sounding better and better to him as he stumbles around the curve.

He looks up and jerks to a stop. There's no one ahead of him! Where did they go? Did they know they were being followed and decide to double back and sneak up on him?

He cautiously looks behind his back, and then he hears faint voices and laughter in the woods to his left. He peers through the trees and can barely detect the group tromping off in the distance. He looks down and sees a small path cutting through the wilderness, so he quickly turns onto the trail and picks up his pace to catch up with them. He's sure now they don't know they're being followed and only decided to take another route back. This trail is obviously off the beaten path with even fewer hikers, which should make his job easier. He smiles to himself and speeds up.

But Dusty is no match for the seasoned hikers ahead of him. He's breathing hard and walking fast, but the group is getting farther and farther away. Adding to his frustration is the fact that the trail is hard to follow. He stops several times when he can't find the path and listens for their voices, and then heads in the direction that he thinks he hears them. Soon he can no longer hear anyone and he realizes he's hopelessly lost. He stops and pulls out his cell phone, but there are no bars and no service.

Dusty walks around trying to locate the trail. How could it just disappear? He hears something to his right and takes off toward the sound, only to find himself in a deep thicket, and still no trail. He turns around and heads back in the direction he came from, or so he thinks, but ends up in thicker woods.

He sits down on a stump to relax for a minute to get his bearings, when he hears some branches crack in the distance. It sounds like someone is coming through the woods toward him and he listens intently. Maybe it's hikers who can help him, but he's got to let them know where he is.

He starts yelling. "Help! I'm over here and I'm lost! Can ya get me outta these woods?"

Silence. Then he hears more twigs crack and branches break. "I'm over here! Help!"

Dusty stands up and looks toward the noise. That's when he discovers it's not hikers coming to his rescue, but a big black bear!

Dusty's eyes widen in shock, and he turns around and hauls ass in the opposite direction. He can hear the bear behind him, but adrenaline is pumping through his body, and he's running like a bat out of hell.

Until his foot hits a rock, and suddenly he's flying through the air over a fallen pine tree. His right leg hits the tree stump, and he hears the familiar sound of a bone breaking before he hits his head on the side of the trunk and blacks out.

FORTY-EIGHT

Two hours later, we're back at the car. The hike was invigorating and fun, and we're all happy and relaxed. When we get back to the marina parking lot, we grab our gear and head for the Moomba.

"What time does Dave get in tonight?" I ask Cynthia.

"I think he said his flight gets in around seven. He has to go through customs, but that shouldn't take too long, so hopefully he'll be at the house by eight thirty or nine. He's going to sleep in and drive up after lunch."

"It'll be good to see him. He's been on the road a lot lately," Catherine notes.

"You'll like him," I tell Mick. "He's Italian too, and full of bullshit."

"Are you saying I'm full of bullshit because I'm Italian?" Mick asks with a grin.

"I think it's in your genes. Just saying."

When we pull up to our pier some time later, I notice that Lola and Pete have already left. Since we're starving, we waste no time heading for the kitchen.

"Oh my gosh, Lola has ribs or a brisket in the oven. It smells heavenly." I'm ecstatic.

"Yep, looks like a brisket to me," Cynthia says as she peeks in the oven.

"And there's potato salad and baked beans in the fridge," Catherine tells us.

"You ladies want a martini while you're nuking the beans and cutting the brisket?" Mick asks.

"Duh!" I roll my eyes at him.

He pinches my cheek and smiles. "I just love when you do that," he tells me and heads for the bar.

I stare at him in surprise, then turn and look at my friends. They both grin and shrug.

Minutes later, we fill our plates, grab our drinks, and head for the front patio, where we can eat and watch the sun sink in the western sky over the lake.

We're laughing and enjoying our food when I get that feeling again, like someone is watching us. I stop eating and slowly glance around behind me. When I turn back, Mick, Catherine, and Cynthia have stopped talking and are watching me

"You've got that look again," Mick tells me. "The one you had back at the Sagebrush this morning."

"I hate to tell you guys this, but I think Clarisse is here. I can...feel her spirit, or her presence, or something."

Catherine leans forward. "How can you tell? Is the hair on the back of your neck standing up? Are you getting goose bumps?"

"No, totally different from that," I tell them. "For one thing, I felt a cold shiver go through my body, and now I smell something musty and kinda rotten in the air. Can you guys smell that?"

"No." Cynthia shakes her head, "I don't smell anything but fresh, mountain air. But ewww! Does that mean Clarisse has BO, or bad breath?"

"I didn't think ghosts had a smell," Catherine says. "I thought all they could do is make the air cold and frigid around them."

"No, I've heard that ghosts can bring special fragrances with them, like roses, lavender, or violets," Cynthia tells us.

"Oh, great. Wouldn't you know I'd get a ghost with bad hygiene and body odor," I mumble as I look around the patio.

"Whatever you do, don't try anything paranormal," Catherine warns. "We have food, dishes, and silverware out here—tons of ammunition she can throw at Mick."

"Let's grab everything and go inside," Mick suggests.

"What if she follows us in the house?" I ask as I quickly snatch up my plate and utensils. "There's lots of stuff for her to toss around in there. Expensive stuff too."

"We've got to figure out a way to communicate with her, and find out why she hates men…or just Mick," Catherine states when we settle inside around the dining room table.

"Why don't we have a séance?" Cynthia suggests.

"Us?" Catherine squeaks. "We don't know anything about séances."

"Wait a minute," I stop them. "We can look it up on the Internet. It can't be that hard, and we've got to do something to stop her assaults on Mick."

"That's true. And you're a medium…in training maybe, but still a medium," Cynthia exclaims. "We'll use the round game table in the den, light candles, and the four of us can hold hands and…do whatever we need to do to communicate with Clarisse."

"Yes, and we can always call Flavia and get her help and input," Catherine says.

"I think this is a great idea," I tell the group. "I'm going to get my laptop." I jump up and a hand suddenly grabs my arm. It's Mick. I look down, and he's staring at the three of us like we've lost our minds.

"Are you fuckin' kidding me?" he asks when he finally talks. "This is the craziest thing I've ever heard, and I've heard a lot this past week. I absolutely refuse to let you do this."

Cynthia, Catherine, and I look at one another, and then I sit down and take Mick's hand.

"Mick, I know it sounds crazy, but we've got to try and communicate with Clarisse." I'm using my soft, convincing voice, hoping to calm him down. "We can't go around not knowing when she's going to strike, and we need to try to find out what she wants. At the very least, we've got to try to persuade her to stop these childish pranks. Besides, what's the worst that could happen? She's already dumped…er, bestowed her precious gifts on me. What more can she do?"

I look deep into Mick's big brown eyes. "Mick, so far she's only done silly, juvenile things to you, but what if she decides to do something serious? You could get hurt, and I'd never forgive myself if something happened to you because of that psycho ghost."

Then I play my trump card. "If at anytime during the séance you don't like something, or you feel any of us are in danger, you can stop it. No questions asked."

Mick studies me, a little skeptically at first, but then he grunts. "Okay, I'll agree to this séance, but only if you three agree to stop it if I say so."

The three of us nod and lock our pinkies together. "We agree," I tell him. "Pinky promise."

FORTY-NINE

"Flavia doesn't answer her phone," Cynthia tells us when she comes into the den some time later. "All I get is her voice mail."

"That's okay. I think I've got all the information we need to do a séance," I tell the group. "We'll have to wing it without her."

"Just the words I want to hear—wing it," Mick tells us dryly.

I hand him the flask of whiskey. "Wing it with this," I tell him. "It'll all be good."

Cynthia lights candles around the den and Catherine turns off the lights. The four of us sit down at the game table, and I notice there's a white tablecloth on it with three candles and a plate of bagels.

"Who did this?" I ask.

"I did," Catherine says. "I read that if we drape the table with a light color, it attracts friendly spirits, and we sure want Clarisse to be friendly tonight."

"Fantastic idea," Mick says.

"And we need at least three lit candles in the middle of the table, and bread or soup—a food offering for the spirits. I thought the bagels would be a good substitute for the bread."

I nod my head. "Alrighty then, let's hold hands, and I'll invite the spirit of Clarisse to join us." We clasp hands and look at one another.

"Umm, maybe we should shut our eyes," I tell them. "It's a little intimidating for me to have you all staring at me."

"Do we need to chant or anything?" Cynthia asks.

"No, we only have to be in one spirit. No skeptics." I look at Mick.

"Then I need one more shot of whiskey," he tells me. He drinks a shot, shakes his head, rolls his shoulders, and winks at me. "I'm ready."

Gee, thanks, Edgar Cayce." Sarcasm is dripping from my voice. "Okay, once again, let's hold hands, shut our eyes, and concentrate."

"Who's Edgar Cayce?" Cynthia asks.

Mick chortles and I give him "the look." "He was a famous spiritualist and medium in the twentieth century," I explain to Cynthia. "Before your time. Now, are we ready to move on?" I look at each of them and Mick holds up one finger.

"What?" I ask with exasperation.

"I need one more shot of whiskey."

"Oh, good grief! Then drink it."

He downs another shot and winks at me again.

"Mick! For God's sake! We need you to be sober here, okay?"

"Hey! I'm sober. I just need a little fortification to do this."

He sits up straight and takes a deep breath as I watch him closely. I swear to God, if he passes out, I won't worry about Clarisse doing him bodily harm—I'll do it myself! But he smiles and closes his eyes.

Once again we clasp hands.

Catherine hiccups and I look up at her.

"Oh my. Did I do that? I'm sorry."

I raise my eyebrows and then I see the shot glass by her hand. "Catherine, dear, have you been drinking shots too?"

"Umm, only a couple of vodka shots to relax me. I'm not tipsy, really. Only relaxed." She reaches down and pulls up a bottle of Grey Goose and puts it on the table.

I look at Cynthia. "What about you?" I ask.

Cynthia looks at me with big eyes. "Me?"

I sigh. "Cynthia, did you have vodka shots too?"

She looks a little guilty. "Only two shots. This is so scary—I needed some fortification too."

"That's what we did—fortify ourselves," Catherine declares.

I look at the three of them, looking at me. "Oh, what the hell. Hand me that bottle of Grey Goose. I need a shot too."

Catherine hands over the vodka, Cynthia gives me the shot glass, and Mick pours. I gulp it down and slam the glass on the table. "Are we ready now?" I ask testily.

They all nod and we clasp hands— again.

I shake my head and take a deep breath. "Dear Clarisse," I begin. "We respectfully ask that you honor us with your presence this evening."

"Amen," Catherine chirps in.

I stop and open my eyes. Catherine has her eyes closed and her head bowed, so I drop my head and continue. "We ask that you come into our presence and honor us this evening by answering our questions. We only want to know you better, Clarisse."

"Yes, sista," Cynthia exclaims.

My eyes shoot open, and I look at Cynthia. Her head is lowered, and I see her lips moving.

"Cynthia, what are you doing?" I ask her.

She lifts her head and looks at me. "Why, I'm chanting. I'm trying to get in the spirit of things."

"Well, please stop. You're making me nervous, okay?"

"Okay," she says softly.

I bow my head. "Clarisse, if you're here, we ask that you make your presence known."

"Hallelujah!" Catherine shouts.

My eyes jerk open, and I see Catherine smiling and weaving in her chair at the same time I hear Mick snore.

"Oh, for Pete's sake," I look at Cynthia. "I think these two are snockered. Can you help me get them to bed?"

"Sure," Cynthia giggles. "Just point the way."

I shake my head. It takes a few minutes, but Cynthia and I get Catherine up to her room and tucked in bed. Then we're downstairs looking at Mick.

"I don't think we can carry him upstairs. Let's see if we can get him over to the couch. We'll pull off his shoes, cover him up with a blanket, and call it good."

It's a struggle, but we manage to get him on the sofa and covered.

"So much for our séance tonight," I tell Cynthia.

"Yep. And God bless us, everyone," she says as we climb the stairs to our rooms.

I sigh. Yep, God bless all my fortified friends.

FIFTY

The next morning I'm surprised to see Mick in the kitchen, all bright-eyed and bushy-tailed. He's grinning from ear to ear as he hands me my cup of coffee when I come through the door.

"Sleep well?" I ask him.

"Sure did. After that long hike and big meal, I was out like a light."

"Not to mention all those shots of whiskey," I add.

He lifts his eyebrows. "You're the one who handed me the bottle. And if you remember, I was winging it." He rubs his chin thoughtfully. "Did you ever get your séance off the ground?"

"Hmph, not hardly. You fell asleep, Catherine was too fortified with her vodka shots to be any help, and Cynthia was running a close second. Jeez, I haven't heard that many amens and hallelujahs since I sang in the church choir."

Mick laughs and reaches over and tousles my hair. "Are the other two ladies still sleeping?" he asks.

"Yeah, I think they're sleeping it off. I should probably be the hangover fairy this morning and take them up some ice water and aspirin."

Mick gets two glasses out of the cabinet, fills them with ice, and hands them to me. I pour filtered water in the glasses and reach for the aspirin bottle. "Be right back," I tell him.

I deliver the water and aspirin and check on my friends, who are both sleeping soundly.

"They may be out till noon," I report when I'm back in the kitchen refilling my coffee cup.

"Good," Mick says, who comes up behind me, puts his hands on my shoulders, and nuzzles the back of my neck. "I've wanted to do this for a long time."

Okay, it's been like, forever since I've had a good-looking, sexy man nuzzle my neck, and I'm melting faster than the wicked witch of the West in *The Wizard of Oz*.

"Oh, my," I gasp. Then I think about how I must look in my wrinkled jammies—a white T-shirt and long, soft, yoga pants— messed-up hair, and no makeup. I almost groan, but then I feel Mick's soft lips kissing my shoulder and working their way up to my ear, and the groan turns to a moan.

As if he's reading my mind, Mick continues to nuzzle and tells me, "You look so dang sexy in the mornings, with your tousled hair and sleepy eyes."

I don't know what to say to that, so I do what I normally do. I shut up.

The next thing I know is he's kissing me, and my arms are around his neck. And as God is my witness, I don't know how it happened, but one minute we're making out in the kitchen, and the next we're rolling in the sheets in his bedroom upstairs. I may be sixty, but I know what good sex is, and damn! This is good sex!

Some time later, I'm lying on my stomach exhausted and content. Mick is lying next to me, slowly running his fingers from my shoulder down to my waist. My eyes are shut and I'm drifting off to Nirvana.

"Constance?" Mick leans over and whispers in my ear.

"Yeah?" I answer softly.

There's silence while I wait for him to say something. I open my eyes and look him square in the face. "If you ask me if it was as good for me as it was for you, I'm going to punch you in the nose."

Mick chuckles and rolls over on his back, pulling me on top of him. "I wasn't going to ask that, but now that you mention it..."

Before I can sputter a word, his lips are on mine, and guess what? Dang if we're not rolling in the sheets again!

After a lot of sheet rolling, we're rumpled and smiling and sitting back down at the kitchen table drinking coffee together.

"What's for breakfast?" I ask Mick. "I'm starving."

"Worked up an appetite, did you?" he asks with a pleased smile.

"You could say that," I tell him with a grin.

He gets up and plants a kiss on the top of my head. "I'm thinking about waffles this morning, if there's a waffle iron up here."

"Everything is up here," I respond and I get up and pull a Belgian waffle iron out of a cabinet and hand it to him. "Will this work?"

"Perfect," he tells me.

"I think I'll go up and shower while you're whipping up some waffle batter."

He puts the waffle iron down. "I think I should come up and help you."

I pick the waffle iron up and push it toward him. "If you come upstairs, we may not make it back down for the rest of the day, and I'm hungry."

He pushes the waffle iron back to me, "I'll make you forget all about food," he says with a sexy growl.

I push the waffle iron back at him. "Oh no, you don't! You've had enough sex for one day, buster. Or at least until tonight."

Mick raises his eyebrows. "Is that a promise?"

"Might be, if you throw in some Belgian waffles to sweeten the deal."

We're standing in the middle of the kitchen holding the waffle iron between us when we hear a throat clear. We turn and see Catherine and Cynthia standing in the doorway watching us with great interest.

"Umm, how long have you been standing there?" I ask my friends.

"Long enough to know that Mick is getting sex tonight, and we're getting Belgian waffles this morning," Catherine exclaims with an excited giggle.

FIFTY-ONE

Dusty comes to several hours later. His leg is throbbing, and he remembers the bottle of painkillers in his pocket and feels around for them. He's relieved to find them still there and pulls the bottle out and shakes three pills in his palm and swallows them dry. He vaguely remembers the bear and looks around, but doesn't hear or see anything. He struggles to a sitting position and pulls his broken leg closer to his body. Fifteen minutes later, the drugs have kicked in and he's lightheaded and giddy.

It's getting dark and he watches as the moon rises over the treetops. He looks around in the moonlight and sees a clump of bushes at the base of a tree close by. It looks like a good spot to hunker down, so he slowly eases his body over until he's able to collapse under the green foliage. It gives him enough protection from the cool, mountain wind, and the pine needles create a soft cushion for his tortured body.

Dusty doesn't know it, but when he tripped over the tree log, he fell right back onto the trail he'd been looking for all afternoon. That's the good news. The bad news is the spot he picked to hunker down in is covered in poison oak.

He falls asleep, and the pain of his broken leg revives him several times during the night to remind him to take more pills. In the haze of his drugs and pain, he dreams about bears, cracking bones, and his body swelling and itching.

FIFTY-TWO

Mick declares his Belgian waffles the best he's ever made. Cynthia and Catherine cheer while I laugh my head off. Hey, I know hands down that those are the best Belgian waffles in the world!

Sometime later I'm on the dock with Mick waiting for Cynthia and Catherine to join us so we can boat over to the marina. We're sitting on the pier in comfortable silence, my bare feet dangling in the water, when Mick points his head toward a flock of ducks headed our way.

"I think some of your friends are coming by to say hi."

"It's that dang animal attraction thing," I murmur as I watch the ducks get closer. "I didn't want to alarm anyone yesterday, but we had a few critters following us on our hike, and I think one of them was a bear."

"Oh, I noticed, although I don't think Cynthia or Catherine did. Is that why you picked up the pace going back?"

"Oh yeah, I was trying to stay ahead of the herd."

The ducks swim up to me and circle around my feet. I reach down, and I'm surprised when a few of them let me pet them on their heads. "Aww, aren't they cute? Look at the little babies—they're adorable."

I see a fish jump out of the water close by. "Hey, do you think fish are attracted to me too?"

"If so, I'm grabbing a fishing pole and we're having fresh trout for dinner."

"Oh no, you don't! I'd hate to think I was the cause of their deaths. Let's eat the fish in the freezer instead. They're already dead." I look around. "Gee, I wonder what else is attracted to me. I hope it doesn't include bugs or snakes."

Mick puts his arm around my shoulder and gives me a hug. "I'm attracted to you, and I hope that doesn't mean I'm in the snake category."

I grin. "You mean like a snake in the grass?"

Several of the ducks swim up and peck Mick on his leg. "Ouch," he exclaims. "Did you see that?"

I look at the ducks in surprise. "Gosh, I think they're trying to protect me. Maybe they think you're hurting me."

Mick stands up and pulls me to my feet. "Hmm, we better go get the Moomba, Snow White, before these ducks get real nasty, or Clarisse shows up."

I grab Mick's hand. "I'm sorry about the ducks, and Clarisse. I don't know what to do about them, but please don't give up on me. I'll try to figure something out."

Mick wraps his arms around me and holds me close. "I'm not going anywhere, sweetheart," he whispers in my ear. "I think you're worth the aggravation."

He called me sweetheart! I sigh in relief, and he grins and kisses me on the forehead. He grabs my hand as we head toward the water garage.

"Besides, I have it from a good source that you're a hard one to catch. I understand you rarely date and usually keep men an arm's length away. I don't know how I lucked out, but I think you're worth fighting ducks and Clarisse for."

"You've been talking to Catherine and Cynthia, and they're prejudiced. But you're right, I don't date, and heck, I don't even know how to flirt, and I certainly don't know how to handle any kind of a relationship either. This is all new to me, Mick."

Mick stops before we get in the Moomba. "Just don't give up on me, okay?"

I look at him in surprise. "Are you kidding? I thought you'd be back in Denver by now—with everything you've had to put up with so far. No, I won't give up on you, Mick Carelli. You're a keeper."

He grins and gives me a bear hug followed by a soft kiss. Which leads to a much longer and deeper kiss. Which leads to...Oh my!

FIFTY-THREE

It's a little after one when we reach the Grand Lake Marina and park the Moomba. Eli is waiting for us on the dock with a big grin on his face. Catherine looks over at me and smiles.

"We're going to have a hot time at the ol' Hideaway tonight," she tells me.

"What do you mean, going to?" I snort. "That place has been smokin' all morning."

Just then we hear a squeal from Cynthia when she spots Dave strolling up to the boat. She jumps out and gives him a big hug, with me and Catherine right behind her. We're laughing and hugging, and when I finally get a chance, I introduce Dave to Eli and Mick.

"Dave, Catherine, and I have known one another since grade school," I explain. "He's like our big brother."

Dave shakes hands and casually looks the two men over.

"Yeah, and I'm protective like a big brother. I knew Cynthia was holding back and not telling me everything, so that's why I decided I better cut my trip short and come home. You ladies need to tell me what's been going on." He looks over at Catherine. "And why you have a bodyguard."

Mick looks at me and raises his eyebrows.

Oh, boy. Confession time for the three Chiquititas.

Cynthia puts her arm through Dave's and leads him toward town. "We'll tell you everything over lunch. Let's have some Mexican food at Pancho & Lefty's." She looks over her shoulder at us. "And big margaritas."

While we wait in line, we enjoy their famous margaritas, and soon we're seated outside on the sunny patio under a huge umbrella.

Dave listens quietly as Cynthia brings him up-to-date on everything. Occasionally he stops her to ask a question, and sometimes Catherine or I interject a comment, but for the most part, he remains silent until she finishes.

It takes longer than I realize to recap what we've been through for the past ten days. Holy crap! Has this been going on for ten days?

We've finished our food and are sipping the last of our margaritas as we watch Dave shake his head in disbelief.

"I can't believe you three decided to come up here alone to hide from this Dusty guy. Thank God your boss sent a bodyguard, Catherine."

"We didn't think Dusty would find out where we were, or would follow us here," I tell Dave. "Catherine was told to lay low for a few weeks, and that's what we were doing."

"They're not real good at lying low," Mick comments. "Or following orders."

Dave chuckles. "Sounds like I got here in the nick of time. You two guys have had your hands full."

"Now wait just a minute," I start, but Mick grabs my hand and pulls me up before I can finish my rant.

"Why don't we head back to the house and change into our swimming suits?" he asks. "I'd like to try out some tubing or skiing behind that Moomba, if there's a wet suit that'll fit me."

Dave can't hide the surprise on his face when he sees Mick put his arm around my shoulders and walk me toward the exit.

"I think there's a lot more going on than you've told me," he tells Cynthia, as he watches Catherine and Eli walk by holding hands.

"There are some things you can't talk about in mixed company," she answers slyly. "I'll tell ya later—when we're alone." She wiggles her eyebrows and smiles as Dave hugs her close and laughs.

When we get to the marina, I stop in and pick up the keys to the pontoon and bring them out to Dave.

"Here, big guy. You know how to handle this monster, so why don't you and Cynthia take her to the house. That way we'll have a boat big enough for all of us to fit in if we decide to go on a picnic, or do a sunset cruise."

I turn to Mick. "If you want, you can bring your rental boat back. There's no sense in keeping it since we'll have two boats at our place. I can follow you back over in the Moomba."

"Sounds like Constance is trying to get you alone—again," Catherine suggests with a grin.

Dave looks at Mick. "Exactly which body are you guarding?" he asks with a smirk. Then he turns and gives me the eye. "I think you've got some explaining to do, sis."

"Dave," I tell him in a serious tone. "Me and Mary Poppins have one thing in common."

"You're both practically perfect in every way?" he asks.

I lift my eyebrows. "Okay, we have two things in common, but the most important one is—we never explain anything," I reply sweetly as I sashay down to the Moomba with my arm around Mick's waist.

"Mary Poppins?" Mick looks down at me with a big smile. "And here all this time I thought you were Snow White."

FIFTY-FOUR

In the early afternoon of July third, three hikers stumble across Dusty. He's half-conscious, delirious with fever, swollen beyond imagination, and mumbling constantly about a bear through his dry, cracked lips. When they realize the serious condition he's in, one hiker takes off for help while the other two stabilize his broken leg, give him water, and get him as comfortable as possible.

Several hours later Dusty is in an ambulance headed back to the hospital in Granby. When they arrive, he's hustled into the ER, where one EMT turns him over to the staff as he runs down his vitals, and another hands Dusty's wallet with his identification and medical cards over to the nurse in charge...a beautiful Cajun woman named Flavia.

FIFTY-FIVE

Later in the day, I'm bouncing around in the Moomba watching Dave and Cynthia hang on for dear life behind the boat as Mick skips their tube across the crystal water of Shadow Mountain Lake. Earlier, Mick and I were on the tube and Dave was driving the boat. I knew right away the ride was going to be a doozie because Dave had that mischievous glint in his eye I knew so well. The same one he had when he was six years old and bombarded me with snowballs on my way home from school when we were in the first grade.

"He's got that look, so watch out," I had warned Mick. "He's going to try to dump us."

And sure enough, he did. Now it's payback time and Mick is working hard to unload our two laughing friends. Seconds later they fall into the water, and we circle around to pick them up.

We pull Dave and Cynthia in the boat and decide to call it a day and a tie, and head for the house.

Catherine and Eli aren't with us because they decided they wanted to ride the ATVs and explore the trails behind the house. Or that's what they told us. More than likely they were exploring the sheets on Catherine's bed.

When we pull up to the pier, Catherine and Eli are waiting for us, and I can tell from the glow on Catherine's happy face I was right about where they went exploring. I bet those ATVs never made it out of the garage.

We strip out of our wet suits, draping them over the patio chairs to dry out, and Catherine and Eli follow us into the house and listen to our tales of daring skill and agility on the tube, in between our peals of laughter and teasing pokes at one another. I can tell right away that all the guys get along and it's a nice feeling to know that everyone is in sync, personality-wise. You'd think Eli, Mick, and Dave were longtime friends like Catherine, Cynthia, and me.

After we change into some dry clothes, the men are in the den making drinks and the women are in the kitchen throwing sandwiches and snacks together from our leftover brisket. Music is playing and we're all eating and talking and trying to decide if we want to go on a sunset cruise or play poker.

"Why can't we do both?" Catherine asks. "Let's go on a sunset cruise and then come back and play poker."

"Or we can play poker while we're on the sunset cruise," Eli suggests.

That gets a loud boo from us women, and he raises his hands in surrender. "On second thought, let's do a short cruise and a long poker game."

Catherine jabs him in the ribs with a finger. "We were thinking about trying another séance tonight if everyone is okay with it."

"Séance?" Dave asks with raised eyebrows. "You had a séance?"

"Let's put it this way, Dave," I tell him. "We tried to have a séance, but Mick and Catherine had a few too many shots and it became more like a revival meeting. Catherine was hollering 'Amen' and 'Hallelujah,' and Mick fell asleep before the preacher even got started."

"Hey, I have enough trouble with Clarisse without giving her an invitation to come in and harass me," Mick defends himself.

"Let's go on our sunset cruise, and we can decide what we want to do when we get back," I suggest as I grab a bottle of wine from the bar and some plastic glasses.

Before we can get out the door, Catherine's cell phone beeps and she looks at the number. "I'm not sure, but I think this is Flavia," she tells us.

Catherine answers, nods her head, and whispers, "It's Flavia."

We wait in the foyer and watch as Catherine listens to Flavia's excited voice over the phone. The expression on Catherine's face changes from a smile to a gasp and then back to a *really* big smile.

"Wait a minute, Flavia. Let me put you on speakerphone." Catherine grabs Cynthia and me and pulls us into the den, with the guys following close behind. "You've got to hear this! You won't believe it," Catherine tells us eagerly.

She puts her phone on the game table and hits a button. "Flavia, I have you on speakerphone now. Tell everyone what you told me."

"Hi, ladies! I have to tell you what happened today. I just got in from work—I'm a nurse in the emergency room at the Granby Hospital, and the EMTs radioed that they were bringing in an injured hiker from Grand Lake Village. You won't believe this, but it was Dusty Galucci! He was hiking on a trail and got lost. From what we could finally get out of him, a bear chased him, and he fell over a tree stump and broke his leg. That was sometime yesterday. He spent the night in the woods and of all things, he fell asleep in some poison oak. He was in bad shape when he came in, but he's stabilized now."

The six of us stare at one another, and then we all break out in big, big grins.

"That's not all," Flavia continues. "His arm was in a cast and he mumbled something about being in the hospital last week. I checked our records, and sure enough, he was treated for a broken arm, but he also had tons of ticks in delicate places, and wasp stings all over his body, and he wouldn't tell anyone how he got them."

"Wait a minute, Flavia," I stop her. "You're telling us Dusty is in the hospital right now with a broken arm *and* a broken leg, *and* he's swelled up with a rash all over his body from poison oak?"

"Yes, ma'am, that's exactly what I'm telling you. The EMTs gave me his ID when they brought him in, and that's how I discovered

226

who he was. So naturally when I examined him, I also did a reading, and I know exactly how he broke his arm and got those ticks and stings. He was spying on you behind your house and climbed in a tree, got tangled up with a wasp's nest, and fell, but not before an army of ticks invaded his privates. It took two nurses several hours to pick all those little buggers off."

Our three men groan behind us. I see Mick grab the whiskey flask and several shot glasses, fill them up and pass them around.

"Our guys are having a hard time digesting that last bit," Cynthia tells her with a grin.

We hear Flavia's soft laugh over the phone. "And then Dusty was following you on a trail yesterday when he got lost, was chased by a bear, tripped, broke his leg, and knocked himself out. That man is a walking disaster and should've never left Denver. He's not what you'd call an outdoors type of guy either. He had dress clothes on, or what was left of them, when they brought him in."

We're all listening to Flavia in stunned silence.

"So in the past week, he's been in the hospital twice with self-inflicted injuries?" Mick asks, shaking his head.

"Yes. He should be released tomorrow or Friday. I've already put a plan in motion to get that contract on you cancelled, Catherine. After I get through with the Galucci family, I don't think they'll bother you anymore."

"What kind of plan?" Catherine asks.

"Let's just say it involves superstition, magic, voodoo, witchcraft, and gossip."

"Oooo, that sounds wicked good," Cynthia tells her.

"Oh, and I got your message about last night. Sorry I missed your call, but I was working late. Did you do a séance?"

"We tried, but ran into a few problems, so we never got it off the ground," I tell her. "We were thinking about trying again tonight."

"Please don't do it without me. Clarisse is a powerful spirit, and you may get into trouble if you're on your own. Can you wait until tomorrow afternoon? I'm working an early shift at the hospital in the morning, but I can drive over when I'm done, and we can do a séance then. And I talked to my sister, Beignet, yesterday. I'll tell you all about our conversation tomorrow if that's okay."

"No problem," Catherine says with a huge smile. "I think we're going to do a little celebrating tonight. Dusty's in the hospital, and I feel safe for the first time in a long time."

"Hey," Mick protests. "You've had a personal bodyguard the whole time you've been up here."

"And a dang good one," Catherine agrees. "But I think it's time you guard a different body, and besides, I think Eli can take over for you now."

We all cheer and whoop, and make plans to pick Flavia up the next day before we hang up. Then I exchange the bottle of wine for a bottle of champagne, and we boogie out the door for our celebration sunset cruise. I know, I know—it's hard to imagine sixty-somethings doing the boogie, but like fine wine and cheese, we get better with age.

FIFTY-SIX

When I wake up the next morning, it's early and I feel strange. As I work the cobwebs out of my brain, I try to remember everything that happened the night before. There was Flavia's call, our sunset cruise, followed by a marathon poker game, and oh yeah! Can't forget that. It's why I'm snuggled up against Mick this morning, and that's why I feel strange. I haven't shared my bed with a man in over ten years.

We're sleeping like two spoons. Mick's arm is resting across my body, holding me tight against him. Actually, it feels kinda cozy and nice, and I snuggle deeper under the covers and let sleep overtake my brain, which thinks too much anyway.

I drift back to sleep, and when I wake up again, I can feel Mick stirring and nuzzling up against me.

"I'm going down to make coffee," he whispers as he kisses my ear.

"Umm," is all I can muster up from my cocoon.

Mick chuckles softly. "Go back to sleep and I'll bring you a cup in a few minutes."

"Snfulggst," I answer.

I hear his quiet laugh as he gets up, and suddenly the bed feels empty.

Sometime later I get a whiff of coffee and raise my head. Mick is standing over me, holding a big cup under my nose. I sit up quickly and grab it out of his hands.

"Oh, thank God. You remembered the cream."

"Being a detective, I tend to notice little things more than the average person."

"Hmmm, I think you're an awesome detective, but an even more awesome bodyguard. And you make an awesome cup of coffee. Thanks."

Mick grins and kisses my forehead. "My pleasure." He sits in the rocker next to the bed and picks up his coffee.

I lean my head back against the bed and look at Mick. Gosh, a girl could get used to this. Waking up in the arms of a good-looking man, with a great laugh, who's a great kisser, and has a great sense of humor. I sigh and sip my hot coffee. There are a lot of greats there.

"I called Samson this morning," Mick tells me.

"Did you tell him what Flavia told us about Dusty?" I ask.

"Yes, I gave him a full report." Mick shakes his head. "This has been the strangest case we've ever been on. It's the first time we didn't have to do anything to the bad guy—just stand by and watch him self-destruct."

"Do you think they'll call off the contract on Catherine?"

Mick grins. "My money's on Flavia. I'm a real believer in the paranormal now."

I narrow my eyes at him, and Mick laughs. "I bet you never thought you'd hear me say that."

Now it's my turn to laugh. "With all the things Clarisse has put you through, I figured she'd make a believer out of you sooner or later. And speaking of Clarisse, I better get up and get dressed. We have a meeting with the grand old lady this afternoon."

I put my cup down and start to get up when Mick reaches over and stops me. "Wait. I think we need to talk about the elephant in the room first."

I sit back and my eyes widen. "What elephant?"

"Our relationship, or fling, or whatever you want to call it. Where are we going from here?"

"Where do you want to go?"

"I don't want to go anywhere. Constance, I want to continue seeing you, and being with you after all this is over, and I need to know how you feel."

I gaze into Mick's dark, brown eyes. "I want to continue seeing you too, if you can stand dealing with Clarisse. We seem to be a package deal at the moment."

Mick stands up and pulls me into his arms. "I'll take the whole package, if you think you can handle an ex-detective with a crazy work schedule."

I nod my head yes as I wrap my arms around his waist. "So, are we making some sort of pact or agreement here?"

Mick lifts my face up to his. "You bet we are. An exclusive relationship."

He kisses me softly and I grin. "Does this mean we're going steady now?"

FIFTY-SEVEN

Mick and I are in the kitchen making breakfast when the others finally stumble in. Okay, Mick is doing the actual cooking, and I'm pouring cups of coffee and passing them out.

"What's for breakfast?" Cynthia asks.

"Scrambled cheesy eggs with hash browns and bacon," Mick tells her.

"Oh, gosh! I just had a thought." Catherine looks sad. "If Flavia's plan is successful and they call off the contract, you'll be going back to Denver. You won't be around to make breakfast for us anymore, and we might not ever see you again."

Mick and I look at each other, and I raise my eyebrows. "Oh, I don't know about that," I say. "I think you'll be seeing a lot of Mick."

Everyone turns and stares at us. Then Catherine and Cynthia let out a whoop, and hug the daylights out of me.

"So, are you saying that all you're going to miss is my cooking?" Mick asks with a big smile.

"No! Of course not." Catherine tries to look insulted. "We've gotten used to having you around, and you've done a good job of protecting us." She comes up and gives him a hug. "But I would like to point out that all the times you've nearly drowned, or been attacked, was because of Constance, not me." She turns and it's my turn to get a hug. "Constance is the one who needs a bodyguard, and I'm so happy it's you."

"I would miss your Lemon Drop Martinis," Cynthia solemnly declares.

"That does it," I proclaim and put a hand on my hip. "He has to stick around if for no other reason than to make our Lemon Drop Martinis."

Mick grabs me, leans me over, and plants a big one on me. When I come up for air, he's grinning from ear to ear. "I think I can do more than make Lemon Drop Martinis."

Catherine and Cynthia are raising their arms and saying, "Woo-hoo" and Eli and Dave are whistling. They're all loud.

"Okay, you guys, show's over," I tell them. I'm a little embarrassed and overwhelmed by Mick's show of affection. Then I grin. Actually, it's kinda nice to have a BF to go along with my BFFs. Something I'll have to get used to.

We finally get down to the business at hand—breakfast—and after we finish and clean up, we head out to the pier.

"How about a morning cruise?" Dave asks.

We all like that idea, so we jump in the pontoon. We're pulling away from the dock when we hear jets overhead.

"Look! It's a flyover by the Air Force Academy," Eli exclaims.

Sure enough, four jets in formation fly over the lake and we wave and cheer.

We cruise around the crowded lake for awhile and then decide to head toward the marina and town. We dock the boat and get to Grand Avenue in time to see the Fourth of July Parade. The street is decorated with flags and banners, and the huge crowd is cheering. There are booths at the park filled with slices of watermelon and apple pie, and we can smell the hamburgers and hot dogs from the vendors' grills all around town.

"Real small-town America," Catherine sighs.

"Yep," Cynthia agrees. "Now let's go shopping! I think I need a Grand Lake T-shirt and some souvenirs."

The men groan.

"We can get some burgers and hot dogs afterward," I suggest.

The men perk up, and we head for the shops.

Much later we're munching on brats and burgers and watching for Flavia.

"If you're looking for someone like Whoopi, forget it," I tell Eli and Dave. "Flavia's a beautiful French Cajun woman."

"Where did you tell her to meet us?" Dave asks.

"At the marina. She said she should be there by one o'clock, and it's almost that time now. Maybe we should mosey on down."

When we get to the coffee shop by the marina, we see Flavia and holler at her. She turns and waves and I hear Dave catch his breath.

"My God," he exclaims, and grabs his chest. "You lied to me. She's a dead ringer for Whoopi Goldberg."

FIFTY-EIGHT

"Ha!" Cynthia pokes Dave in the side. "She's a real sweetheart, and she'll know everything about you just by shaking your hand."

"No secrets from her, that's for sure," Mick warns them.

We hug Flavia, and introduce her to Dave and Eli, who cautiously extend their hands. She starts laughing and hugs them instead.

"You've obviously heard about my talents," she teases.

"Your reputation does precede you," Eli laughs sheepishly.

"Your secrets are safe with me." She turns and looks at Mick. "You're looking well, in spite of Clarisse's mischievous attempts at doing you bodily harm. What's the old girl been up to?"

"Not too much since we last saw you," he tells her. "She showed up at the ice-cream shop the other day and snatched up our cones, along with everyone else's, and tried to throw them at me. But we were able to get out in the nick of time. The cones hit the door instead."

"Close call." Flavia shakes her head.

"I was trying out my mind reading abilities the day of the ice-cream cone attack," I tell her. "I sensed someone following us and I was afraid it was Dusty. Turns out it was Clarisse. I've sensed her around several times since then, but I keep my paranormal gifts under tight wraps so she doesn't have a chance to do anything. We thought if we did a séance, we could find out what she wants, or why she keeps picking on Mick."

"It's worth a try, although I'm afraid Clarisse is nothing more than a big troublemaker. She likes working her magic and causing havoc, so as long as she can work through you, she's one happy bitch witch."

Mick cuts his eyes at me, and I know what he's thinking. Seriously, I know what he's thinking! I've caused a little havoc myself these past few days, and Clarisse and I are a matched pair. Two bitch witches. I know he's teasing, but I raise my eyebrows and give him "the look," daring him to say anything. He doesn't. Smart man. Instead he grins and grabs my hand as we all stroll down to the pontoon.

When we get to the house, I show Flavia around so she can decide which room to use for our séance.

"The game table in the den would be the best place, if we can all fit around it," she tells me.

"I think we can make that work. It's an octagonal shape and fairly large."

We pull extra chairs in from the kitchen, I close the blinds in the den, Cynthia lights all the candles around the room, and once again, Catherine puts a white cloth on the table.

"You've done your homework," Flavia tells us. "Good work."

"Before we start, can you tell us what's going on with Dusty?" Catherine asks.

Flavia gets a wicked look on her face. "Oh yes, let me tell you about Dusty." She leans forward and lowers her voice conspiratorially. "I have several good friends who are nurses at the hospital, and they know all about my psychic abilities. When I told them what was going on with Catherine, and the contract out on her, and who Dusty was, they were more than willing to help."

Flavia's smile widens as she turns toward Catherine. "They've been spilling gossip around Dusty—making sure he hears that I'm a voodoo queen from New Orleans, and that I can read minds and put hexes on evil people. Very exaggerated stories, of course."

We all nod in agreement and mumble, "Of course."

"While Dusty's been fading in and out of consciousness, two of my friends make sure they're in his room talking about me," Flavia continues. "One of them even came up with a story about how I put a horrible hex on a hit man from Denver who was trying to kill a friend of mine and caused him to have some bad accidents."

Flavia's eyes are twinkling, and we're all sitting breathless, taking in her every word. "And of course I solidified the gossip by letting a few things slip out while I was taking his vitals this morning." Flavia giggles. "I asked him if he found the binoculars he lost when he fell out of the pine tree after he shot the wasp's nest. His eyes got huge and his face turned white. But when I asked him when his cousin, Frankie Two

Toes DeFalco, was coming to pick him up, I thought he was going to pass out."

"Who is Frankie Two Toes DeFalco?" Catherine asks.

"Rocky Galucci's grandson and right-hand man," Mick answers. "They call him Two Toes because when he was a teenager, he accidentally dropped a loaded pistol and shot two of his toes off."

Cynthia shakes her head. "Only in America."

"How did you know about Frankie?" I ask Flavia.

"I picked it up when I was taking Dusty's blood pressure. He's an easy man to read. His cousin called him earlier this morning, about an hour before I got in."

We're all smiling, and I notice that Dave and Eli are looking at Flavia a little amazed. They'll get used to it.

"When I got off duty today, I stopped by Dusty's room on my way out," Flavia continues. "I told him I'd be back to check on him again tomorrow. I know for a fact he was thrilled to hear that."

"Do you think they'll call the contract off?" Catherine asks.

"Oh, trust me, that's a done deal. The icing on the cake is happening right about now," Flavia looks at her watch. "One of my friends is telling Dusty about my great-great-great-grandmother, Marie Laveau, the famous voodoo queen of New Orleans. When he finds out about her, your contract will be history."

241

We all look at Flavia with bewildered expressions.

Marie Laveau? Who the heck is Marie Laveau?

I have an eerie feeling we're going to find out real soon.

FIFTY-NINE

We're all sitting in the semi-darkness looking at Flavia, trying to digest everything she's told us so far.

"Okay, séance time," she declares, pulling us out of our stupor. "Let's all hold hands. Feel free to keep your eyes open or closed, whatever you're comfortable with. The key is to empty your minds of everything and concentrate on the name Clarisse." Flavia stops and looks over at Eli and Dave. "You two have never experienced our magnificent and malevolent little witch-ghost, so whatever happens, do what I tell you, okay?"

They nod their heads, and we hold hands. I close my eyes and concentrate on Clarisse. I'm a little nervous, but Mick gently squeezes my hand, and I squeeze back. Then we listen to Flavia call for Clarisse

"Clarisse," she quietly whispers. "We're asking you to come into our group. We're anxious to talk to you. We know you're a revered and respected spirit, so with much humbleness, we ask you to join us."

I think Flavia's laying it on a little thick, but within seconds I hear Clarisse's familiar cackle.

"She's here," I mumble softly to the others since I know they can't hear her.

"Thank you for coming," Flavia continues. Her voice is quiet, and I can tell by her touch that she's part of the spirit world right now. "Clarisse, would you honor us by answering some questions? We need to know why you have come back, why you need Constance to be the vessel for your gifts, and why you don't like Mick."

I feel a shiver down my back, and then I hear Clarisse's ethereal voice as she answers, "A lot of questions." There's silence for several seconds and then she continues. "I don't like men. They're useless beings and cause much trouble in the spirit world," she hisses. "And I've come back because I miss my powers, miss using them, miss the amusement they bring to me."

"Why don't you like men?" Flavia asks reverently.

"Oh, bah! They're worthless and not trustworthy," Clarisse answers with an indignant huff.

"But not all men are the same, Clarisse," I tell her. I can't help it—I have to interrupt. "Mick hasn't done anything to you. Why do you pick on him?"

"You're wrong, all men are the same," Clarisse insists. "They'll pledge their love and loyalty, but will leave you with nothing once they have your heart, and your money."

Aha! Some dude in the nineteenth century duped her, and now she's making all men pay for his sins.

"Did he take all your money?" Flavia asks with sadness in her voice.

"Almost all. I managed to squirrel away a small sum to pay for my potions and magic, and to keep me alive. But he left me in squalor and poverty, turned his back on me, he did, for a much younger and beautiful woman. He took all my inheritance, and because he was a man, he could do it."

Okay, now I feel her pain. I can sympathize with her, and thoughts of my ex and his new wife creep into my mind. Except my ex didn't waltz off with all our assets and money. Times were different for women a hundred or more years ago. Now we have a more equitable legal system, for the most part. It may not be perfect, but it's tons better than what women had before.

"That bastard." I can't help myself. The words come out of my mouth before I can stop them.

I hear Clarisse laugh softly. "Yes, the love of my life deserted me, but I made him pay, oh yes. I made him suffer, and his new lover even more."

Suddenly my sympathy quickly turns to revulsion, and I don't like the tone of her voice at all.

"What did you do?" I ask.

"What didn't I do?" Clarisse laughs wickedly. "I perfected my paranormal gifts and used them to make their lives miserable. They died in pain and in even greater poverty than I was in. And may their souls rest in hell."

Okay. I'm not a big fan of my ex, but hey, sooner or later a girl's gotta move on, get a life, and find some happiness. Revenge is so over-rated. And right now Clarisse is scaring the bejesus out of me.

"Hey there, Clarisse. I know you got a bad deal, and your ex was real bug spit, but ya know, times have changed. Mick here is not like that at all." I'm trying some female logic to win Clarisse over to my side. "Can you give him a break? Ya know, this isn't gonna work out between you and me if you keep picking on him."

"You wish," Clarisse cackles, and the hair rises on the back of my neck. "If he chooses to stay around, he'll pay the consequences."

So much for female logic, and I certainly don't like her witch's logic. And what is it with all this cackling? Can't she just laugh or giggle like a normal ghost? Or maybe give us a little moan every once in awhile?

"Clarisse!" Flavia interrupts with a firm voice. "Constance is a mother and grandmother, and she's not equipped, nor does she have the desire to be the vessel of your great and numerous gifts. You need to find another receptacle immediately."

I didn't think Clarisse was going to like that remark, but then, a girl's gotta do what a girl's gotta do.

"What," Clarisse hisses. "You dare defy me?"

I think we made Clarisse a little angry. Okay, very angry, because the next thing I know, there's a strong wind blowing through the room, and we're all staring at couch pillows, candles, playing cards, poker chips, pictures, and sundry other items whirling around our heads. That's the mild part. The ugly part is when lemons and glasses from the bar start bombarding Mick and the rest of us.

"Yikes! Duck under the table," Flavia yells at us.

We're diving for cover, but Catherine's not fast enough, and I look up to see a lemon sail across the room and smack her in the face. She grabs her head and sinks to the floor with a moan.

That does it. All of a sudden I'm sick and tired of Clarisse and her gifts and her little temper tantrums. It's one thing to annoy the hell out of Mick with lemonade and ice-cream cones, but it's another to intentionally hurt one of my best friends.

"Stop," I shout as I stand up and yes, totally defy Clarisse. "I'm so done with you, bitch! Get out of here and leave me alone. If you think you can ruin my life and hurt my friends, you're wrong." I raise my arm in a fist of defiance. "I promise you I will never use any of your paranormal gifts again. We're through, Clarisse."

I'm so hopping mad, I can't see straight. I don't even notice when the wind stops and all the flying objects fall to the floor, because I'm on my hands and knees crawling toward Catherine.

"Are you okay?" I ask when I'm by her side. By then Eli has her in his arms and we're all gathering around to inspect the damage.

Catherine groans and opens her eyes. "Good Lord, what just happened?" she asks.

"You got hit by a flying lemon," I tell her.

"You've got to be kidding me," she exclaims, and sits up straighter, holding her eye. "Are you telling me that after nearly two weeks of worrying about Dusty and some hit man whacking me, I get knocked out by a flying lemon?"

Cynthia and I look at each other, and then we can't help it. We're so relieved Catherine's okay and bitching about a lemon that all we can do is grab her in a big hug and start laughing.

"You're gonna have one big shiner there, girlfriend," Cynthia tells her.

By then Catherine is laughing too and hugging us back. "Did you get rid of Clarisse?" she asks me.

"For the time being," I tell her. "I may have to go to New Orleans and visit Flavia's sister to get the job done completely, but that witch-bitch is history, as far as I'm concerned."

"You'll have to tell us everything that happened because we only got one side of the conversation," Cynthia tells me.

Mick kneels down by us with an ice pack in his hands and gently puts it on Catherine's eye. "Sorry I couldn't take that lemon for you," he tells her with a grin.

"Yeah, and what's up with that anyway?" Catherine asks indignantly. "I thought bodyguards were supposed to take the hits for their clients."

"Bullets," Mick tells her sweetly. "We take the bullets for our clients, not the lemons. Sorry, sweetheart."

SIXTY

Dusty Galucci is lying in a hospital bed with his broken right leg raised on a pillow, and his broken left arm resting on his chest. He's trying to take a nap, but all he can think about is that nurse, the voodoo queen, and scratching the welts all over his body. Which he can't do because his hands and fingers are wrapped up in gauze and rubber gloves to keep him from scratching.

The door to his room swings open and he lets out a small, frightened scream. In walks his cousin, Frankie.

"What'sa matter with you?" Frankie asks as he walks toward Dusty's bed. "Christ! You look like shit."

Frankie shakes his head and pulls up a chair close to the bed. He rests his big arms on the bed rails and looks Dusty over. Then he looks his cousin in the eye. "I hate to tell ya, cuz, but word is goin' round that you've been tryin' to commit suicide to get outta doin' this hit."

"What?" Dusty's eyes widen in shock. "That's a lie. I'm in here because of that voodoo witch who's put a hex on me."

Frankie raises his eyebrows. "Wha'cha talkin' about? What hex? What voodoo witch?"

"The one I've been hearin' about for the past two days! Everyone is always talkin' about her and who's she got a hex on now, or who's she gonna do next."

Frankie grins at Dusty and shakes his head. "I think you been takin' too much of them hospital drugs. Your brain's warped, fried, shriveled up."

Dusty sinks his head in his pillow and groans. "You don't understand. She's a nurse and she's been in here. In this room, talkin' to me and tellin' me things that she shouldn't know. Shit! She asked me when you were comin' to pick me up, and I never told anyone you called this morning and was comin' up here. How'd she know that, huh? And she called ya by your name, Frankie Two Toes!"

Frankie sits up with interest. "She knew I was comin' here and she knew my name? How'd she know that?"

Dusty shakes his head in frustration. "That's what I'm tellin' you! This broad knows stuff, man. And then I heard two nurses talkin' this afternoon about how's she comes from a long line of voodoo queens in Louisiana."

Frankie frowns and rubs his chin with his hand. "You're tellin' me you're not tryin' to commit suicide? That all this was caused by some hex put on you? I dunno, man."

Dusty pulls himself up with his good arm and grabs his cousin's shirt. "You know me, Frankie. I'm too chicken to whack myself—I'd never do that. But you know hexes and spells are for real, right? Remember Grandma Belladonna? She had the 'eye,' man. She put a hex on Uncle Tony Fioni, and his nuts turned black and fell off! You remember that?"

Frankie leans back in his chair and his frown deepens. "Yeah, I remember all about Uncle Tony. Poor bastard."

"This voodoo queen is for real, man. She's comin' back tomorrow, and you gotta get me outta here before she does. She knows I'm the one sent to do the hit on that James broad. That's why she put the hexes on me, and that's how I broke my arm and leg. She's gonna kill me unless we call off that hit, man, I'm tellin' ya."

Dusty closes his eyes and lies back down with a loud moan.

Frankie looks at him a minute, then pulls out his cell phone and walks toward the door.

"Who ya calling?" Dusty asks nervously.

"Grandpa Rocky. I'm gonna tell him what's goin' on—that you're not tryin' to commit suicide, and that ya got some voodoo witch on your back. This whole deal with the James broad is old news. And besides, your ma is bitchin' about getting' you back to Denver. She's drivin' Grandpa nuts, thinkin' you're tryin' to commit suicide. He's sick and tired of listenin' to her, and told me to call off the hit and come get you. Otherwise she'll never shut up."

Dusty shakes his head in relief. "Thank God. After you finish talkin' to Uncle Rocky, call the nurse and let's get the hell outta here."

SIXTY-ONE

After our séance, we take Flavia to her car in Grand Lake, and then come back to the house. Cynthia, Catherine, and I clean up the broken glass and smashed lemons in the den while the men prep our food for dinner. When we finish, Mick finds enough good lemons to make us some Lemon Drop Martinis. Dave makes us appetizers, and all three guys insist we relax on the patio and take it easy for the rest of the day. They grill steaks and veggies for dinner, and then they clear the dishes and clean up the kitchen. It feels good to be pampered. I'm personally drained from the séance, and still seething from Clarisse's little temper tantrum. Catherine definitely has a shiner, but on her it looks good. She's such a trooper.

Now we're all relaxing together, watching the magic around the lake as the sun slowly sinks in the west. We're sitting around in pairs waiting for dark and for the fireworks to start. The ones in the sky, not the ones in the bedroom.

Cynthia looks over at me and grins. "'I'm so done with you, bitch'? I can't believe you said that to Clarisse."

I sigh and lean back in my lounge chair. "I am done with her. And she is a bitch."

Mick softly laughs beside me. He's holding my hand as we sit side by side, and he brings it to his lips and gently kisses my fingertips. "I didn't know you could raise your

253

voice so loud," he says. "You were mad as hell. You sure scared the bejesus out of me."

I roll my eyes at him. "Yeah, right, you big, tough detective. I bet nothing scares you. And you forget I'm a mother and a grandmother, so yes, I can raise my voice and get loud."

"What did Clarisse tell you?" Catherine asks.

She and Eli are sharing a lounge chair together and suddenly that looks cozy to me. I look over, and Dave and Cynthia are sharing one too. I get up and plop down by a surprised Mick.

"Scoot over, sugar lips, and I'll tell you what she said," I tell him. He grins and puts his arm around me.

When I'm all cozy and comfy, I tell my story.

"It seems Clarisse married a scumbag. She had an inheritance, but some gold digger made her fall in love with him, and then once they were married, he kicked her out, took her money, and ran off with a younger woman. Evidently in those days a woman didn't have any rights, and once she married, everything became her husband's property. She managed to squeak by, learned witchcraft and made potions. When she got powerful enough, she used her paranormal abilities against her ex and his lover. She said they died in pain and poverty."

"That's kinda sad, really," Catherine says. "Not the revenge part, but the fact that she fell in love and it wasn't returned."

"Yeah, well, when I told her it wasn't going to work between her and me if she kept

254

picking on Mick, she started threatening me. She told me if Mick chose to stick around, he would pay the consequences. That's when Flavia interrupted and told her to find someone else to give her gifts to."

"And that's when all hell broke loose," Dave comments in a quiet voice. "What all do we have to replace in the house? Besides the bar glasses?"

"Lemons," I tell him with a smile. "Mick barely had enough for our martinis tonight."

"Maybe you and Sugar Lips can go get more tomorrow," Cynthia suggests with a grin.

We hear a beep, and Mick get ups and pulls his cell phone out of his pocket as he walks toward the pier. We're all quiet as we watch the night creep in and wait for Mick to return.

In a minute he's back with a big smile on his face. "That was Samson," he tells us. "It seems Dusty Galucci was picked up from Granby Hospital late this afternoon by his cousin, Frankie Two Toes, and taken back to Denver. But the big news is—the contract on Catherine's been called off."

Cynthia, Catherine, and I sit up and look at one another. For two seconds. Then we jump up and go in for the group hug, with Mick in the middle. We're laughing and screaming and hugging, and by then Eli and Dave are on their feet doing the happy dance with us.

I run into the house and grab bottles of chilled champagne and plastic glasses, since the real glasses are broken, and bring them back to the patio.

We're still laughing and hugging as we watch Dave and Eli pop the corks and Mick fill our glasses.

And with perfect timing, the fireworks start in the middle of Grand Lake and light up the sky with a loud boom.

In the midst of the red, white, and blue rockets and flares in the dark Colorado night, Catherine, Cynthia, and I raise our glasses and say our toast, "Here's to your liver, lover."

EPILOGUE

On a warm evening in late July, Catherine, Cynthia, and I are sitting on the patio at Gordon Biersch with Lemon Drop Martinis.

"What else did Flavia tell you?" Catherine asks while she sips her martini.

I sigh. "She told me that her sister, Beignet, will help me get rid of Clarisse, but I have to go to Louisiana. You remember when she told us her sister never leaves New Orleans? Well, she doesn't, and I have to go to her. Flavia tried to talk her into coming up here for a visit, but no dice."

"When do you think you'll go?" Cynthia asks.

"I'm not sure. I'd kinda like to wait until it cools down a little, if it ever cools down in that part of the country."

"Is Mick going with you?" Catherine asks with a twinkle in her eye.

"No, he can't leave Denver right now. He's on a big case that's going to tie him up till the end of the year. I don't think I can wait that long. Can you two come with me?"

"I can if you wait until October. I have some vacation time I need to use up before the end of the year, but I can't leave until then," Catherine tells me.

"October would be perfect. What about you, Cynthia? Can you make it too?"

"Sure can. I'd love to find out more about this Marie Laveau while we're down there."

"October it is then. Let's toast to it!" I lift my glass to do our toast, and a premonition hits me.

In the haze of my vision, I see a tall, well-built man standing on the banks of a big river. He's dressed in eighteenth-century clothes—black tight pants, high black boots, and a white shirt with ruffles on his cuffs and collar that's open in the front. Did I mention the tight, black pants?

I'm close enough to see his dark, curly chest hair peeking out in the opening of his shirt, and I catch a glimpse of his long, black hair under a pirate's hat with a large white plume. He looks straight at me and smiles. Then he takes off his hat with a flourish and bows deeply.

My vision ends, and I sit back in my chair and gasp. "I just had a premonition," I tell my two friends. "And for the first time, I think it was about me."

"We could tell something was going on. Suddenly you're talking and then we could tell you weren't with us anymore," Catherine tells me. "That was the longest premonition you've ever had. What happened?"

"I'm not sure, but either I'm going to be in a movie with Johnny Depp, one of those *Pirates of the Caribbean* flicks, or I'm going to meet someone who looks a lot like Jack Sparrow. It was odd. This guy was dressed up like a pirate and he looked straight at me, took off his hat, and bowed. I swear he could see me! And I believe he was standing on the banks of the Mississippi River."

"Maybe it's someone you're going to meet in New Orleans," Cynthia suggests.

"Possibly, but I don't understand why he was dressed in a pirate's costume. They don't wear clothes like that in New Orleans anymore, except in movies. I can't figure it out."

"Let's toast to our upcoming trip, and your clandestine rendezvous with a tall, handsome pirate," Catherine says, raising her glass.

"Okay, but promise me you won't say anything to Mick about the pirate. I don't understand what he's all about, and I'm sure Mick won't either."

"We promise," Cynthia and Catherine say together.

We lift our glasses, and do our toast.

Scared Hitless is a fictional story. All of the characters that appear in this book, and the events that take place, are works of the imagination. Any similarity to real persons and actual events are purely coincidental and not intended by the author.